Prairie People

Prairie People

A Short Story Collection

DILLON HAMILTON

RESOURCE *Publications* · Eugene, Oregon

PRAIRIE PEOPLE
A Short Story Collection

Resource Publications
An Imprint of Wipf and Stock Publishers
199 W. 8th Ave., Suite 3
Eugene, OR 97401

www.wipfandstock.com

PAPERBACK ISBN: 978-1-5326-9959-7
HARDCOVER ISBN: 978-1-5326-9960-3
EBOOK ISBN: 978-1-5326-9961-0

Manufactured in the U.S.A.   JANUARY 2, 2020

To my beloved wife, Heather, and son, Cillian.

Contents

Preface

This collection of short stories was a response to my old professor's challenge to "write what I know." The advice was humbly received but sadly, not heeded until a year later.

I thought, knowing little about the world and having no expertise in any academic field or discipline, that I wouldn't be able to establish believable or creditable characters. I felt that my education, which I consider to be meager in the face of all I intend to learn, was insufficient to provide the proper amount of focus and thought to any project of fiction, great or small. I thought, having been raised on a baseball diamond, that baseball was the only thing I truly knew. Largely, this was true, but I failed to see baseball had been a conduit for observations across many of the ecoregions in Oklahoma, as well as the Great Plains. Outside of writing, the only knowledge and skills I have practiced to a certain level of adequacy can be most useful on a mound or at a plate. I failed to appreciate, but do appreciate now, how a game, at its supreme use can teach many virtues to young men, brought me before characters like those in these short stories.

Though, this is not a work about baseball. In fact, baseball is mentioned few times beyond this preface. But the opportunities it presented to me to meet and observe loveable souls on the prairie could not be understated. I have learned to admire them and believe their character and way of life deserve a kind and honest recording. I hope you enjoy my humble and brief attempt at such a recording.

Oklahoma Needs an Ocean

Eviction had always been on the table for *Knuckle's* and since the arrival of the more violent earthquakes Vince had no choice but to concede to all demands. He quit listening to the assessor's rambling after she proclaimed the century-old structure was "unsound." She muttered something about a foundational shift and a weakened roof, but Vince had already wandered out of earshot to his favorite corner of the diner. The corner where he would sit for the few hours before opening with a tea or coffee, depending upon the season, and watch the old and new characters of downtown go about their business. He imagined the days when he was a young customer in the diner, before he had graduated, where he would wait for Bethany in the same corner next to the same window. The cold seeped through the poorly-caulked corner next to his leg as it had then, but these days there was no Bethany to warm him with her presence.

Vince picked up the salt shaker and tapped a dash onto the backside of his hand. Some of the salt tumbled onto the table for two, but most landed between the black and gray hair on the back of his hand—pure white jewels upon leather. He blew a concentrated and strong stream of breath at the spilled salt, sending it into the air to fall to the floor and be trampled by his regulars for one last day of service.

"Did you get that, Vince?" his sister Joan asked.

Vince had not paid attention to any of the conversation since hearing the verdict for his beloved building was condemnation and the sentence was death. "What?" he asked, listlessly.

"Out by noon tomorrow and Sharon will need *all* the keys. We can't risk someone else stepping into this death trap once we leave. Got it?"

Vince nodded, pursed his lips, and turned down the corners of his mouth like a frustrated cartoon character.

Joan dressed her voice in her 'momma' tone. "I'm serious, Vincent. No funny business. I know how sentimental you get with this place."

Vince used the same response as before, adding a "Mmm hmm," for clarification.

Joan returned to her conversation with the assessor, claiming, "Those frackers will pay for this." Vince surveyed Main Street for a few more moments before walking back to the kitchen, where his employees and coffee would be waiting. He had seventy-five feet to decide how he should announce that they would be out of a job by the end of service. He had seventy-five feet to decide whether he would add bourbon or cream to his dark roast. He had seventy-five feet until he reached the saloon-style kitchen doors where he said a short prayer each time he exited in hopes that Bethany would be sitting in their corner.

The doors moaned for help on their hinges. No matter how much lubricant he applied Vince could never make them happy. An unopened fifth of bourbon stood resolute on a steel counter next to a stout and steaming cup of coffee. Two figures waited at the end of the long polished kitchen, which seemed to reflect all the light that it could into Vince's face—a testament to their thorough late-night cleanings.

"Tomorrow, huh?" a young woman with neon pink and purple hair asked.

Vince removed the bourbon's plastic covering, uncorked the bottle, and poured the caramel-colored liquor until the mixture brimmed and overflowed the rim of the clay mug. Streams stained the eggshell paint exterior and ran over the cold counter, fogging the metal around the hot pool. "My cup overfloweth," Vince muttered.

"Out of context, Vince," the young man next to the girl said. His jeans looked starched stiff and his tone was as sharp as the knives at his workstation, which never failed to cut clean through produce.

Vince forced a smile, but his hopeless stare and languid eyelids betrayed him. He wished for their own sensibilities that he could have lied to them. He never wanted them to be miserable at *Knuckle's* if he could help it. "Tomorrow."

"Where are we moving to?" Karleigh asked, knowing there would be no moving, but wanting to trap Vince in a guilty corner over her joblessness.

Vince took a gulp from his mug, thinking the whiskey would have cooled the coffee sufficiently to do so. The coffee burned his tongue and the alcohol stung the wound.

Fitting, Vince thought.

He coughed, cleared his scalded throat, and said flatly, "We won't be moving."

Karleigh struggled to untie her apron, eventually electing to yank the knotted garment over her head. She slammed the apron onto the stained concrete floor with a resounding whish. "How long have you known that you would be sending Steven and me into a frantic job search?"

Vince stubbornly gulped down another mouthful of punishment. "Today."

Karleigh's attitude softened slightly toward her boss, but continued, "Why don't you have a Plan B, Vince? Are you just giving up?"

"I'm retiring," Vince said.

Classic rock music played through the overhead sound system as it was scheduled to, every morning at nine, to mentally prepare Vince and his staff for another day of service. Vince found a spare towel to soak up the coffee and bourbon he had spilled.

"We have the perfect setup to move. There are a few buildings in town that would be more than enough. In fact, they're better than this dump. This should have been demolished years ago." Karleigh waved her hands and tossed her colorful head about dramatically.

Vince normally appreciated the color she brought to the kitchen, but found it more than a small annoyance on this particular morning. He squeezed the soiled towel until it eked the adult coffee back onto the counter.

Karleigh continued. "You could at least think about going down the road to Guthrie or even Stillwater. Do you realize how easy it would be to pay off a building if you served a bunch of drunk Cowboy fans on game days? I know two frat guys that could eat three Uppercuts in one sitting."

"I'm not retiring because I have no other options. I'm retiring because that's what I want. The building is condemned, I won't be able to sell it. At best, I'll be able to salvage some from the industrial equipment, but it's nearly as old as I am."

Karleigh nodded, not from approval or an acceptance that it should be so, but in rage. "Yeah, that's it. Let's just give it up. Give it up and leave your workers to fend for themselves."

Vince, unsurprised by Karleigh's normal outbursts, sensed an amplified angst in her voice. "What's wrong with you?" Vince asked. "I can't do anything about this. It's out of my control." He tried to temper his usual gruffness and leaned against the counter to appear less menacing.

"You're just quitting! You're giving up!" she yelled. Her shouts echoed off the brick and patchy stucco walls.

"Everything okay back there?" Joan shouted from the front.

"Just doing some HR work back here. We're fine," Vince replied.

He shoved himself off the counter, reverting to stubborn and surly Vince. Passing cars reflected morning light into Vince's squinted eyes and weary brow.

"I don't mind a different opinion on what I should do, but this isn't personal, Karleigh. I happen to like you brats, which is more than I can say about most of the kids that have worked here. Yes, I have the money and time to start over somewhere else. Yes, it may be more lucrative and beneficial long term, but I no longer have the will to serve sandwiches to day laborers, construction crews, and gossiping townsfolk, okay?"

Karleigh kicked her apron into the steel cabinets below the counter and barged past Vince to the rear exit of the building.

Vince turned back to Steven and asked, "Do you feel the same way?"

Steven shook his head. "I've enjoyed working here, but I go off to basic in a month. This just gives me more time to help my Grandpa around the golf course. He pays better than you anyway." Steven laughed and tended to the skillet, sautéing onions for their renowned, and Vince's favorite, Backhand sandwich.

Vince refrained from immediately chasing after Karleigh. In his limited experience with his nieces, although it helped them to talk and reason through their feelings, he found that young women of Karleigh's temperament required time to regain a sense of normalcy before any discussion would be constructive. He watched the stoplight sway outside over the cobblestone street. Clouds of dust occasionally collided with the storefront windows when stronger gusts pushed down the hill like an unseen tsunami. Steven whistled and worked. He carried a mournful tune that accompanied the outdoor scene well.

Vince drew regular gulps from his mug, which had cooled significantly but still stung his tongue like the regular cleansing of an open wound. Outside, characters he had known for decades fought over the sidewalk against the wind with defiant strides, determined to reach their destination in spite of the westerly howls, much like their ancestors had done a century or more before them. Hair and hoods hid most of their faces, but Vince knew their moods by the state of their shoulders before they ever entered his sandwich shop. Four pairs of confident and jolly shoulders approached the entrance to *Knuckle's* like they had nearly every morning since its opening.

卵

"I call the coffee maker," Jack said, raising his hand before the rest of his friends had their chance to claim anything.

Vince pointed at his lively friend. "Sold to the lover of riddles and all things tweed."

Jack tipped his gray Donegal beret to the other men at the table. His satin eyebrows rose proudly with the announcement of his winning bid.

"So they're just going to tear this thing down? Didn't the city offer you something ludicrous to transform this into a historical site? They were going to give you that empty patch with the gravel parking lot across from the school, weren't they?" a man with a normally dense gut and light brain asked, not realizing his accurate hindsight added a sting to Vince's growing emotional wound.

Vince held up his hands in protest. "Now Dave, I know this will be the first time you've had the chance to tell me that you told me so, but there's no way you foresaw this. Earthquakes in Oklahoma?"

"I sure did." Dave lifted his coffee mug like a gavel and let it fall with a thud on the unbalanced table. The rest of the men let out a collective and unbelieving groan. "It's true and none of you are willing to admit it." Dave spoke smugly, as a master would to a servant. "You fellas ought to listen more often."

Another man, wrapped in a brown denim jacket with an even denser gut than Dave, waved off Dave's claim to right prophecy. "This coming from the guy who supposedly took a photo of Bigfoot back in the seventies, but 'lost' the film."

Dave crossed his arms, resentful at first, but then smiled. "It's true, Laramie. I lost the film, but I would much rather lose a photo of Bigfoot than the hair on my head."

Laramie grasped the wool beanie next to his coffee and covered his bald head and small cauliflower ears. His surroundings and mood subsequently dimmed.

All laughed with the exception of the sullen friend who sat directly opposite Vince, yet to enter the conversation. He was clean shaven with straight, coarse hair, like porcupine quills, holding a ball cap just off the surface of his scalp. His eyes, like the contrast between the depths of a high prairie sky above hazed horizons, were icy orbs set in tanned leather. "You knew she would never come back," he said. The others nodded their agreement.

Vince's heart grew morose, but he smiled, concealing his hopelessness from his friends. "Yeah, she never had a reason to," Vince said.

The wise and weathered figure leaned forward. He caressed his mug with both hands and pulled the steaming liquid under his nose, inhaling the notes of the roast, which were bitter and burnt. "No, she had reason to come back, but that reason could not overcome who she was, Vince. Your personalities fit well. The best parts of you grew when you were around each other, but your purposes for your own lives killed whatever you had."

The barricade around Vince's emotions fell with the last of the silent strikes of siege weapons that had bombarded him all morning—all his life. Tears were not fitting for finally losing hope in a romanticized fantasy he had built for Bethany and himself. Grief over the death of his most treasured fiction would require a quick burial under the infertile rocks of a soft nihilism. "It'll be just fine, fellas. I'll retire and let Uncle Sam pay for my meds until the ol' liver fails. Talk about purpose, eh Jerry?" he said with a curt, ironic laugh.

Jerry searched the depths of his coffee, inhaling their fumes again. "None of us can pretend we know what it's like, Vince. We still have our jobs for the day and our families to go to at night, but the consensus among all honest men, including us, is that the motive behind starting something like you have here with *Knuckle's* rarely ends with the fulfillment of your original goals."

Dave, Laramie, and Jack nodded in somber agreement, again. Vince fumbled with the handle of his mug that held an alarming amount of cream and sugar with very little coffee, a saccharine overcorrection to the bite of piping hot coffee and whiskey.

Vince cleared his throat. "So you think me being sentimental about this place has led *Knuckle's* to its end."

"No, that's not what I'm saying. I'm saying—what I think we all would say—that your reason for buying the building and creating this business has produced interesting and meaningful fruit, fruit that can easily lead to new purpose."

Vince glanced across the room at *their* corner. He could almost conjure her figure. He imagined her in a tank top with the rays of a brutish summer illuminating her freckled shoulders. He almost heard the laughs they would have had over a beer and his retelling of boyish acts committed during military adventures abroad. She would have especially enjoyed the stories from Germany.

"We were in contact almost the entire time," Vince began, to his friends' surprise. "She never bothered to tell me the letters would stop or that she was leaving town. There wasn't a hint that anything would change, or that anything would be different between us when I came back. I still feel like I'm in the same position I was in those first few weeks back. I vowed to keep the seat across from me open as long as I could."

"You do know that she'll never be the one to take that seat though, right?" Jerry asked. He hoped Vince understood the reality that Bethany's presence and companionship were no longer a possibility.

Vince nodded. He understood Jerry only intended to reason him toward letting the fiction go, even though that fiction made for a most pleasing and satisfying end to his efforts. Thankful for his friends' care, he preferred to avoid their pity.

"How much cash did you say you wanted to give me this morning, Jack?" Vince asked.

Jack revealed a fresh deck of playing cards from his inner jacket pocket, still encased in plastic wrapping. "Whatever I take from all you suckers is going into my donation for a *Knuckle's Two,*" Jack said, hoping the conversations and card games would end only with their deaths.

Jack dealt the first hand of stud. Dave, Laramie, and Jack folded and tossed their tear-stained cards into the center of the table after Jerry called Vince's first bluff.

✿

As Vince had suspected, word spread of *Knuckle's* closing and loyal customers ordered their favorites or tried the new sandwiches they had never ordered in fear that this would be their last chance to do so. Vince answered all questions about his future and the restaurant's future with an indifferent, "We'll see," knowing most of his customers to be the town's alarmists and he did not want to run out of ingredients on the last day, which looked likely already. His friends continued their poker game and bought sandwiches with the cash he had lost to them. He had never been more satisfied with losing out of a poker game so quickly.

Vince enjoyed his self-appointed responsibility of waiting at his own diner. Rushing around kept him nimble and warm when winter came, and appropriately trim during the putrid summer months. He would have admitted he lived to play jokes on each table at least once during their meal. Devising fresh pranks and jokes satisfied his playful nature that he could no longer entertain around his nieces, who had grown too cool for his mirth. Happy customers fueled his feet and they would all have agreed Vince deserved tips, but he never took any, telling them, "If you have that much to give, buy another sandwich and take it home."

On this last day, Vince continued in his practiced fashion. His smiles, jokes, steps, and quick service ran on happy habits, lifting the day out of its general gloom. He checked the kitchen with regular glances and was relieved to see Karleigh's bright hair bouncing from counter to counter in the kitchen, even though he endured her glare each time he retrieved a sandwich from her station. He waited for a knife to be flung at his back as he left to serve, but enjoyed the protection of the saloon doors slamming behind him.

Steven hustled through the lunch rush with expert precision and focus, reminding Vince of a gunner mate he once knew, who could clean and check four guns to any other sailor's one.

Hectic lunch orders came and went. The sun sent familiar flairs and shadows across the checkered tile floor. Vince, who had been cleaning, halted his work when he noticed the sun had wholly dropped below the Byzantine green and gold-rimmed awning. It was time for breaks.

He and Karleigh normally convened over her afternoon cigarette breaks and his fourth cup of coffee, but Karleigh quit smoking after her first pregnancy and Vince cut back on his caffeine intake after advice from multiple specialists. Vince decided it was still best to avoid Karleigh and her attitude. It was a battle he might have fought in her early years at *Knuckle's*, but any argument or method of persuasion he could use now seemed frivolous.

After returning his ancient broom with its duct tape-mended handle and its dustpan to the janitorial closet, he returned to *their* corner. He thought it would be nice to enjoy one last spring sunset. His seat always faced directly to the west. The sunset at this particular time of year aligned with his view down Main Street almost perfectly, making it nightmarish for any westward travelers, but pleasing to any stationary lover of prairie sunsets.

Vince took his seat and wiped the exhaustion from his eyes and the sweaty grime from his brow. With eyes closed, he let the powerful warmth of window-filtered rays wash over his poorly circulated hands. Once an irritable setting because it distorted his view of Bethany's face, giving him only her silhouette and voice to admire, Vince now welcomed the sun's restoration. He would sit here, at *their* table, until the view beyond his closed lids suddenly darkened and his hands cooled behind the arrival of a shadow.

A woman's silhouette, much like young Bethany's in size and proportion, replaced the sun's onslaught. The light bent through the horizon and retained its rich color around the woman, tracing her in delightful pinks, lively oranges, and a purple that royalty could never find but always coveted for their robes. The woman sat upright and crossed her legs with relaxed professionalism. Her shoulders, carved and leveled by a master sculptor, did not budge with her heavy breathing. Vince expected long hair to adorn her, but realized the pinks and purples shone in all their glory through her short but still feminine cut.

"I'm sorry, Vince," Karleigh said.

Startled and not ready to forgive her, Vince said, "I thought you'd be chucking some of the broken concrete at the grease trap out back right about now."

Karleigh laughed. "I'm not eighteen anymore, Vince. I can't act like my daughter and cry or throw things every time I don't get my way. Although, occasionally, I do it anyway."

Vince nodded and smiled. He appreciated the woman she had become, but could not help feeling the disappointment of it not being Bethany across from him. His friends had revealed the plot holes in his fantasy, but Karleigh's presence forced him to read the reality.

"I shouldn't have acted the way I did." She paused and leaned forward shyly. "Zach doesn't want it known, but he was laid off at the tire plant because of some new automation. He's ashamed, but I promised him to continue working so he could try to get more commissions for city murals and that sort of thing. I think he can do a wonderful job and make a living. It's just exhausting trying to get started. People don't appreciate talents like his, at least not around here, ya know? Anyway, I'm also emotional because I found out this morning we'll be having our second child."

Vince's focus on pointless dreams broke and he listened with sympathy and intention.

Karleigh continued, "I just know me losing this job will crush Zach. He already feels guilty for not bringing in any income. And of course, he'll miss the sandwiches I get to bring home. It was all those things at once that triggered that old habit inside me." She shook her head and gazed at her folded hands in her lap. "I was even searching for a pack of cigarettes in my car when I barged out. The point is, I'm extremely sorry, Vince. It was no way to act and I've been doing my best to control myself all day in hopes that you'll give me a good reference when I start job searching."

With Karleigh's admission, Vince experienced the warmth he once found in Bethany's presence. He now surmised that he never harbored a self-defining love and care for Bethany, but in Bethany, he found a reason to work toward a goal that would gratify all his desires of service toward another. Bethany left for reasons she never made clear and never experienced the fullness and benefit of Vince's care, but in her absence Karleigh reaped all that he had meant for Bethany. In spite of her confrontational nature and behavior, Karleigh appreciated the ways in which Vince had served her and her family. Vince knew she treasured him over any paycheck that he could provide her, but the loss of a dear friend, which she had in Vince, she bemoaned.

He could tell Karleigh wanted to say more, but he could not let her apologize again. He stared directly into the sun, whose crown melted into the pitch edge of the horizon. The automated Edison bulbs that hung above each table from the tiled ceiling began to brighten, stealing away the sun's prominence and filling the room with a copper glow. Vince noticed Karleigh must have cried before she had joined him in the corner. Her high cheekbones had been rubbed raw by a jacket sleeve and the soft rims of her eyelids were irritated. Vince surprised her with a deep and clear voice.

"Does Zach do indoor murals as well, or is he more of an outside guy?" Vince asked.

Initially off-put by the question, Karleigh failed to understand its connection to their current conversation. "He can do it all. And what he doesn't know he studies until he's comfortable with it. He can create inside and outside. I'm not sure he has a preference as long as he's getting paid."

Vince leaned forward and fought away a smile. "That's good. I'll need him to come with me to look at buildings, starting tomorrow. He'll have a better eye for a good wall than I will."

Karleigh's face, now fully illuminated, contorted with confusion. "Why would he . . ." A restored joy and contentedness came to her expression and voice. "Are you serious or is this another joke you're trying to make?"

"I'm serious. I want him to paint and I need you to continue in the kitchen. You'll have to train someone new when Steven leaves and they'll need to be prepared for your maternity leave, but we'll cross that bridge when we happen upon it. Do you accept those terms?"

Unable to speak through her breathless rejoicing, Karleigh simply nodded.

Annoyed by the amount of tears shed during the day, Vince turned back to the sunset. "Another masterpiece in the sky. Always thought we had the prettiest sunsets in the world here. I think Oklahoma needs an ocean to go with our sunsets," he said.

Karleigh replied with a feeble voice, "I'll make sure Zach paints one for you."

The PK

When Ryan's father received the call to take the pastorate at a small Baptist church in Blaine County, Oklahoma, Ryan felt the familiar unease of settling into another small town and school. His nausea waxed and waned with thoughts of struggling to make friends and earn the trust of the adults of the new church, who always seemed on the lookout for reasons to call him or his younger siblings "rebellious."

The shame and guilt associated with rebellion followed him like one of his younger siblings, ready to charge and accuse him for any infraction. His father assured him the task to "remain blameless" in the sight of the congregation would be even more difficult in this small town where the church he intended to lead recently had the great number of forty added to their congregation thanks to a dispute and division over doctrine at the nearby Methodist church.

"The new ones won't enjoy my preaching and teaching, but we must make them enjoy us, as a family," his father said of the Methodists on their way to his first Sunday morning as lead pastor.

Stanley Brewer preached four sermons in the new brick building, funded by the First Baptists, before they decided he had the right pitch, tone, and style for their tastes. His Tennessee twang reminded them of the voices constantly playing over their radios from the Oklahoma City stations. They thought his stiff and immaculately clean suits fit him especially well when he shouted over the edge of the pulpit, "Washed by the blood of the Lamb!" And it helped that he supported the strong united front against alcohol consumption by all Baptists in town. Although, Ryan knew his father would take a nip or two of rye on colder nights, an offense of hypocrisy and betrayal neither his congregates nor his fellow Tennesseans could ever forgive.

First Sundays were tryouts, where the skills and attitudes of the preacher's kids were tested, analyzed, and judged by the whole of the congregation and their children. Ryan's performance would be dissected by most families on their rides home, beginning with the parents in the front seat. The parents compared his posture with his Scripture memory, and his singing of the hymns with his attentiveness during the sermon. It was common, and many times important, to have their children's perspectives entered into the conversation for consideration. They would meditate upon his actions until they reached their verdict before setting their minds on the casserole waiting for them in the oven at home. Some would even consider his performance long after the last square of casserole had been devoured. He appreciated the extra contemplation these congregants took. They were the ones most likely to look upon his first impression with a gracious heart.

Being the eldest of four brothers, Ryan carried a tremendous responsibility to bear the family image and keep it blameless for his younger brothers. If any of them had, Heaven forbid, started a fight, lied to an especially communicative church lady—who had no interest in covering a multitude of sins but instead announced it to everyone with the exception of the boys' authorities—or didn't participate during Sunday School, Ryan atoned for their actions in many ways. He bore this burden well and labored through his responsibilities with the steadiness and strength of a good ox.

Thankful for the air conditioning during his first Sunday School class, Ryan expected his four-year-old twin brothers, Kaleb and Keller, to keep their suit jackets on for at least thirty minutes but, sadly, they surprised him and had apparently removed their jackets within the first few moments of the lesson and waved them above their heads, calling themselves "ropin' cowboys."

Ryan, who had answered most of the memory verses with near perfection, had learned only too late of his brothers' hooliganism. Had he known, he would not have allowed the others in his class to answer any questions, hoping a better first impression of his knowledge of the Word would cancel out the actions of his brothers in the eyes of the congregation.

Somewhere between his class and their family pew in the sanctuary, Ryan picked up the breathless retelling of his brothers' chicanery and more than a few varying versions that were recited in King James English.

The twins sat on their hands in the oak pews with matching neckties and grimaces. Little baby Isaac cooed in Jeana Brewer's cradled arms. Her eyes loomed like a spring prairie storm over the twins and scrutinized their every breath. Jeana welcomed her eldest with a smile. "I heard good things about your first day, Ryan. Mrs. Elderberry says you have the finest memory of Scripture she has ever seen from a ten-year-old."

Ryan nodded dutifully and avoided the doubled indignation of his brothers' sideways glances. If they were back in Indiana, he would have brought their sourness to his mother's attention, but this was a first Sunday and his family could not afford a discipline trip to the lobby on the first Sunday. It would brand all the Brewer boys as troublemakers and limit their freedoms wherever they went. Public discipline always raised the standards by which a preacher's kid ought to act. Every time his brothers received the love of a good swatting, his own tie was tied tighter and his hairdo required more saliva to counteract their barbarity.

The adults greeted each other with the joy of Friday night's win and the embarrassment of Saturday night's near loss. It was a consensus among both Baptists and Methodists that the local high school team was a much steadier and more sufficient source of pride than the still heavily supported college team.

Having mastered the idol of basketball in Indiana, Ryan doubted his ability to deliver for the idol of Oklahoma—football. His long, wiry frame chanced collapse under all those pads and if the equipment didn't break him, he was sure an outside linebacker would.

Football talk died under the sound of pounding out-of-tune piano keys and the familiar first notes to the first verse of *Abide With Me*. His father joined them in the front pew after greeting the last of the deacons. He placed his hand on Ryan's shoulder and squeezed with the love of a pleased father. Ryan attempted to match the depth and strength of his father's voice through all four songs and twelve verses.

As the music leader blessed the preaching, Ryan marveled through squinted eyes at his father's ability to step silently up the wooden steps, place his note-filled, sheepskin Bible on the pulpit without sound, and straighten his suit with a stern tug of his jacket.

❧

Though it was late fall, the bi-monthly potluck was held indoors due to heat concerns for elderly members. Ryan allowed his mother to fill his plate with many questionable-looking glass-pan-cooked dishes that tasted like broccoli even though they didn't all contain broccoli. He said thank you each time a spatula plopped another mound of sticky mush on his floral-pattern paper plate. He dined next to the twins and a chatty deacon, who had an endless amount of concerns for Pastor Brewer about the order of service and timing of the invitation. "We could get more salvations and rededications every Sunday," he said. Kind as the deacon was to voice his concerns directly to his father, Ryan wished the balding man had waited to finish chewing his food before asking questions or raising concerns. He could not afford, neither could their family's first Sunday impression have afforded, to have loud smacking and snorting come from his general direction. He rushed eating through the bland goops, disposed of his cutlery and dish, and asked his mother to let him join the other kids in the back yard to play.

Knowing the heat would cause him to take it off anyway, Jeana removed his jacket, tie, and white dress shirt, and rolled his trouser hems to his knees. "I'm not spending hours rubbing out your stains," she said, before releasing him. Jeana normally would have laid a strict perimeter on her child's activities, but the chatty deacon's wife distracted her with scheduling meetings for morning coffee with the ladies of the church.

New to the building and its strange style of minimal windows with a view of the outdoors, Ryan found a side exit near some of the Sunday School rooms for younger children, where the twins most assuredly had gathered their posse and went for a rebellious ride. He shook his head, remembering their actions, but was proud of the way they had responded after their mother's stern correction.

He opened the door cautiously, but the dry heat and wind blew back the door, dragging Ryan back with it. He gradually fought the door to a close, making sure to hear the door latch behind him before walking toward the back yard and into a ferocious south wind. Waves of powdery dust hovered over the sidewalk that surrounded the building's exterior, covering his shined leather dress shoes with a thin dusty film.

He turned the corner to find a group of children fully ensconced in their game of football. A few of the younger siblings, who were naturally barred from playing because of age or size, watched longingly as the action ebbed and flowed to their left and right. Ryan picked out a boy, not much bigger than the twins, to talk to. He wore oddly thick and stiff jeans that were too short for his height and allowed the lime green shaft of his cowboy boots to peak out with every step he took.

The young boy introduced himself as Samson Henry Elderberry. "I like football," Samson said, pushing curly blond locks away from his eyes. "That's my brother, Norris." Samson pointed at the ball carrier with similar blond curls, only they contained more dust and sweat. Ryan recognized Norris as one of the kids coming from the fifth grade Sunday School class. Four defenders struggled to tackle Norris before he breached the makeshift goal line that one of the children had clearly dug out with the heel of their boot. Celebration and childish taunting followed the triumph of a touchdown.

"Yay!" Samson shouted.

"Is Mrs. Elderberry your mom? The one that teaches the fourth grade class."

Samson shrugged. "I don't know if she teaches, but that's my mommy's name."

Ryan nodded. Hopeless the conversation could move forward with much fruit, Ryan pretended to be enthralled by the action. The sandy gusts blasted the backside of the building and all spectators watched through squinted eyes.

Suddenly a portly woman with a slow cooker resting on her hip burst through the back door of the church and shouted, "Hunter Bailey Aldrich! What have I said about tackle football?" Her voice pierced through the unrelenting wind. Ryan recognized her voice as the stalwart soprano that had sang from one of the back pews, overpowering and carrying the congregation. All the children stopped their play and looked to a well-insulated boy for his response.

"You said I can't unless it's Saturday and I've got my pads on."

"Yes sir. That's correct. Now get your rear and your football back in this church before I get Daddy," she shouted. Hunter scooped up his ball that the previous carrier had dropped in fright and scurried up to the church and past his mother before a kick with her heel could land on his backside.

"He's in big trouble," Samson whispered.

Dejected and confused by the abrupt ending of their football game, the children broke into groups of three or four, going their separate ways in search of more acceptable mischiefs.

The three sweatiest and most active football players, including Samson's brother Norris, marched toward him. Ryan shuddered inwardly. He struggled to relate and make new friends with peers because they could read him better than most adults. Adults were easy to pacify and please. Ryan learned at a very young age to comply with the adults and most of his secret thoughts and fears would go unnoticed, but peers wanted much more than he was willing to give.

They introduced themselves as Norris Elderberry, Kaitlynn Huss, and Uwe Werner. Ryan giggled at the pronunciation of the last boy's name, but was deterred by a quick cut of Uwe's eyes. "Sorry," Ryan mumbled.

"So you're the new PK?" Kaitlynn asked. Her nut brown hair was braided close to the scalp and her dark eyes looked close enough to see Ryan's pores.

"PK?" Ryan asked.

"Preacher's kid," Norris said. His sweaty blond hair stuck to his face in spite of the wind that threatened to blow all their little bodies down. "It's short for "preacher's kid." The last PK was a tattletale. Are you a tattletale?"

Thinking critically about the question, Ryan tried to recall an occasion he had needlessly brought another peer's offenses to the adults in authority, but couldn't think of any. He shook his head.

"Good. No one likes a tattletale. Where are you from?" Uwe asked.

"We came from Indiana," Ryan answered.

Kaitlynn leaned forward and squeezed his bicep.

His muscle rolled between her fingers and cramped. "Ow!"

"You any good at football?" Kaitlynn asked.

"I haven't played much. We played basketball in Indiana," Ryan said, rubbing his bicep.

Kaitlynn scoffed.

Norris squinted and sneezed out prairie dust. He wiped his nose with the back of his plaid sleeve and asked, "You pretty fast?"

Ryan nodded. He had once outrun every challenger at a county fair near their church in Indiana and decided he was justified in calling himself fast.

"He'll be good at football," Norris said to the group and turned back to Ryan. "It ain't real hard. You just gotta be tougher and meaner than you are in basketball. Plus, you don't have to practice shooting all the time."

"You like baseball?" Uwe asked, excitedly.

Ryan nodded, smiling. His desire to affirm as many of their preferences as possible was being fulfilled. Taking an errant application of his father's earlier sermon, Ryan attempted to be all things for all his peers in order that he may win a few of his peers to himself as friends.

"Who cares about baseball? It's boring," Kaitlynn said.

"I'll remember that the next time Daddy gets extra tickets to a Rangers game. Ryan can use your ticket since baseball is obviously too *boring* for you," Uwe said, slapping the dust from his jeans. It billowed like a cloud of brushfire smoke, suspended in the air for a moment, then carried away on the wind, adding to the general haze of the day.

"I'm talking about the baseball *you* guys play," Kaitlynn recovered.

Uwe raised an eyebrow. "What's that supposed to mean?"

"Never mind. Leave it alone, Uwe," Norris said.

Ryan viewed Norris as the leader of their group, not only because Kaitlynn and Uwe listened to every word he had to say, but also because Norris had some of the same leadership qualities he'd seen in his father. Both postured themselves toward their friends in a manner that communicated protection and service. Norris suggested and executed the group's mutual desire for physical fun and exploration, a foreign but interesting group goal to Ryan.

As he had in every other congregation, Ryan strove to graft himself into groups that would serve his purpose for good first impressions. Norris and Samson belonged to his Sunday School teacher. Kaitlynn shared the same last name as one of the deacons. Ryan prayed that, assuming he continued to charm the group, the relation was close enough that Kaitlynn could have the deacon praising the "PKs" before nightfall. And Uwe would be Ryan's vehicle to carry news of good first impressions toward the laymen, as he had memorized most of the deacons' last names and found nothing close to Werner residing in his memory.

All but Ryan were slapping the dust from their clothes. Even little Samson imitated his brother, smacking his coarse dark denim in vain with his tiny hands. They tidied themselves enough to avoid corporal punishment, hoping their mothers might even be gracious to the point of skipping a monotone lecture about cleanliness being next to Godliness and just washing their Sunday best.

"What's next?" Uwe asked the group. Kaitlynn shrugged. Norris spat into the wind and watched it carry his loogie a few yards away, disappearing into the wilted and faded Bermuda grass. He squatted and looked around, as if the drought-stricken landscape would provide an answer. The others watched him quietly. Norris stood suddenly and sprinted to the corner of the church and faced Highway 51 with the south wind at his back. Curls still stuck to his damp cheeks but most of his hair had dried, and Ryan could not help but see the similarities between his hair and the goldenrod that leaned away from the gusts in the pastures next to the church. The group grew encouraged, hopeful, and even gleeful as they noticed Norris's smile through his windblown hair.

The wind suddenly ceased and the atmosphere that had reminded Ryan of a blow dryer felt more like his visits to the dentist, where the glare and heat from the light were almost enough to make him panic.

Norris's hair fell straight and he turned toward the group like a conquistador at the prow of some great ship as if he was the first to catch sight of some golden city before the rest of his crew. He shouted. "Hey, PK! You ever been to the top of a grain bin?"

🙣

The wind that had rushed past them in the morning to get to Kansas reversed its course to look for warmer regions in Texas. Winter arrived annually in Blaine County like the new kid who was thrust into classes with strangers in the middle of a school year and couldn't feel comfortable with himself until he cracked a few lips and made noses bleed.

Ryan felt his lips chapping and he reached reflexively for his lip balm in his jacket pocket that wasn't there. He bit his lip, frustrated by the inconvenience and looked back across the highway at the church entrance. He could have made it back before Norris made it to the top of the bin ladder, but Kaitlynn, directly disobeying Norris's command of "one person on the ladder at a time" shoved Ryan's chest into the second rung and guided his sweating palms to clasp the third. "Come on," she demanded.

Ryan licked his lips and stared up at Norris's fearless feet. Norris did not rush his progress, nor did he scale the bin nervously, but hit each rung with his feet and hands almost rhythmically. The metal ladder chilled the sweat on Ryan's palms and the north wind made him more wishful for his jacket than he had ever been. He shivered.

"Let's go! We've only got fifteen minutes before our parents will start looking for us to go home," Uwe said, looking at his cartoon-themed wristwatch.

Kaitlynn rolled her eyes. "That thing is always off. It's PK's Dad's first Sunday and I bet my dad and the rest of the deacons will keep him trapped and talking until dinner time about how to get the water and electric bills down."

Uwe laughed. "Wanna know how to get the water bill down at a Baptist church?"

Kaitlynn sensed another worthless Werner joke. "Ugh! How, Uwe?" she asked in a patronizing tone.

"Get rid of the coffee maker."

Kaitlynn buried the beginnings of a smile that betrayed obvious amusement. "Get better jokes, Uwe."

Norris shouted down. "That's a pretty good one, Uwe. That's the first joke you've told that made sense to me."

Pleased, Uwe smirked at Kaitlynn. "Hmmm."

Kaitlynn rolled her eyes again. This time her irises disappeared completely behind her upper eyelid.

"What are you waiting for, PK? Quit staring at me and get up that ladder!" she squealed.

Ryan pulled himself to the next rung and the next. He matched Norris's pace until one fourth of the way up, heavy shivers and fear slowed his pace by half. Norris watched from over the edge of the bin, beckoning Ryan up the ladder with the wave of his hand.

"I ain't waiting all day, PK," Kaitlynn called from below.

Ryan was acquainted with his fear of heights enough to know that focusing on the next step helped him combat the reality of how nauseatingly high from the ground he actually was. Kaitlynn continued her jeers, which fueled Ryan's ascent. Not that her comments drove him to a sense of determination or anger, but they were welcome distractions from his predicament and clarified the narrative he hoped she would relay to her father, Deacon Huss.

Ryan found the top rung much earlier than he assumed he would. The metal of the giant bin whined and moaned under the onslaught of northerly winds that rivaled their southerly counterparts from minutes earlier. Ryan pulled himself over the edge, where the ladder continued diagonally toward the access hatch. Norris had already made his way onto the metal bridge between bins, suspended fifty feet over First Street. Ryan edged his way toward the hatch until his feet no longer dangled over the edge. The sun warmed his back and the ladder held the sun's residual heat like a fajita skillet. Ryan lounged there for a few comfortable moments, appreciating the warmth he had found bothersome only moments ago.

"Come on, PK. You gotta move before Kaitlynn gets to the top and she's getting close," Norris said. He watched his group's progress at an angle from the bridge. He coached, encouraged, and, in the case of Uwe, scolded them as they made their way to the top.

Ryan struggled with the fear of having to close the empty, and apparently slippery, space between the sure steadiness of the ladder and the bridge. Norris's prints left in the dusty coating showed obvious marks of slippage, his hand marks smudged a frightening distance down the top of the bin. The combination of the north wind and fear stood Ryan's hair on end.

"Hurry up, PK! She's about to be right on top of you," Norris warned.

Ryan heard Samson's faint and squeaky voice from the surface. "Can I come up too, Norris?"

"No, stay where you're at! We'll come down soon." Norris sounded like a parent concerned that his son's natural impatience and curiosity would harm him. "You be lookout, Sammy!" Norris hoped it would be a worthy consolation for his younger brother.

"I'm Samson Henry Elderberry!" Samson yelled in defiance of his brother's command, but he obeyed reluctantly.

"Thanks, Sammy," Norris yelled through a chuckle.

Samson closed his fists, threw them down at his sides, and stomped the dust beneath him.

Ryan, distracted by the Elderberry brothers' conversation and determined to provide a good first impression to the deacon's daughter, edged away from the ladder and onto the slick conical surface of the grain bin. The worn leather soles of his dress shoes provided no friction to use, but the heels were made of a gummy rubber that worked well to hold him near the access hatch. He shimmied toward the open side of the bridge, where three grated metal steps led to the bridge's runway.

"That's it," Norris said, filling Ryan's need for encouragement and distraction from the obvious danger of the situation. "Almost here!"

Ryan used the ribs between the paneled sheets of metal as hand holds and his heels held their grip until his foot caught the first stair to the bridge. He urgently joined Norris, already dreading the dicey shimmy back across to the ladder to get down.

"Not bad, PK," Kaitlynn muttered from the top rung of the ladder. She squatted at the top and gripped the lip of the access hatch. Leaning her head and shoulders away from the cap of the access hatch and transfer auger, she shuffled along the lip and made it to the bridge more quickly than Norris and Ryan had.

Uwe employed a combination of Ryan's and Kaitlynn's methods, using the lip for his grip but moving over the metal in a prone position. His trip was easy and uneventful. Ryan marveled at the others' apparent lack of fear and wondered if all Oklahomans were this brave. If this brand of courage was a statewide phenomenon, he would have to spend most of his school days proving his valor.

"Let's go to the bin across the street," Norris suggested. Kaitlynn and Uwe nodded their agreement. Ryan remained quiet.

The bridge creaked, a high tone under the constant pressure of the wind. The distant squeal of a rusted windmill irked Ryan like his dad grinding the lawnmower blades to a sharp edge. His sense of discomfort returned as the triumph of reaching the bridge faded. The holes in the grated bridge looked much larger to him now as they traveled over First Street. Ryan's heart pounded under his thin shirt, a sheen of sweat breaking out over his chilled skin. His already unstable knees shook with vigor. Kaitlynn and Uwe followed him in his slow progress. He gripped the railing in fear that the platform could not hold their combined weight. He could at least delay his fall by clinging to the railing until his strength failed.

His fear mounted but he pressed on, determined to leave the group with a positive first impression.

Norris arrived at the other end of the bridge, knocked on the cap of the access hatch and shouted, "That was easy!" The low echoing din produced by Norris's knuckles drifted away with the strongest winds of the day.

Ryan's progress halted. He stopped in the middle of the bridge, shaking uncontrollably and frozen in fear. His legs felt leaden and a strange tingle enveloped them. His grip on the rails was so sure not even he could remove his hands.

"What's wrong now?" Kaitlynn whined.

"I can see the Jacobson's combines from here." Uwe spoke through chattering teeth.

Ryan's stomach strained and seemed to fold in on itself with the same heat and force as a burning barn. The rotund bins moaned and rattled. Dust, sweeping in from fields and lands he had never seen, stung and blasted against his exposed skin.

Losing all faith in Ryan, Kaitlynn petitioned Norris, who walked briskly down another bridge. "Will you come get this chicken, Norris? He's blocking our path!"

Ryan heard Norris huff with derision, but he could not wrestle his attention away from the street below him. He felt the eeriness that came with suspecting he was destined for a high velocity collision with the windswept street. The sturdiness of the bridge could not prevent it, his new friends could not help in any way, and his fear-frozen body would be more likely to cause a fall rather than avoid one. He elected to remain where he was at all costs. He would not fall if he just stayed put. His first impression, which he thought had been established quite well before the bridge, would be more sullied by a fall than by staying put.

Norris, who had rushed back to his friends, perturbed and unsympathetic for Ryan's fears, chose a very patient and parental tone when dealing with the new PK. "What's the deal, PK?" he asked.

Ryan let his head hang lower, hiding the tears that now flowed halfway down his cheeks and fell, disappearing in the windy haze of the street below. He didn't answer Norris. Shame and guilt enveloped him and accused his conscience of cowardice. He knew fear was only natural at these heights for someone his age, but refusal to take steps to remove himself from that fearful situation or train oneself not to fear was cowardice, especially when it could affect the well-being of his new friends.

Norris stepped closer to Ryan, within arm's reach. "You two get down," Norris commanded Uwe and Kaitlynn.

"But we only just got up here! Why should we let some *sissy* make us go down?" Kaitlynn protested.

Norris did not tolerate her nonsense. "Go! Now! Get Pastor Stanley."

Uwe obeyed and Kaitlynn squealed with all her wrath, but dutifully followed Uwe back down the ladder. Norris supervised their descent and watched them scurry across the empty highway.

Ryan, agonizing over his cowardice yet crippled with fear, felt his exhausted arms begin to weaken. He had emptied himself of tears. His feet ached and the feeling in his legs had all but left him. His shortened breaths lacked the rich air supply he needed, coating his mouth and nostrils with the dull dust that had spent centuries being tossed around the prairie.

"I used to be afraid of football," Norris said.

Ryan looked up and felt the strain he had placed on his neck by hanging his head. "What?" he asked, confused by the seemingly unconnected admission.

"I was afraid of getting hit. I hated the feeling that I might get hurt."

"You aren't afraid to get hit anymore." Ryan recalled the way Norris seemed to look for contact wherever he could find it on the field earlier that afternoon.

Norris chuckled. "I still am afraid of getting hit. At least, afraid of getting hit really hard and not being ready for it."

"What changed?" Ryan asked.

"My dad told me to protect myself."

"How did you do that?"

"Well, you can't get hit if you hit them first." Norris smiled and placed a hand on Ryan's arm. "I'm going to switch places with you and you're going to follow me down, okay?"

Ryan nodded and marveled at his own natural trust for a boy he had met only minutes before. Norris pulled Ryan's stiffened arm from the rail, slipped past him, and let go of his arm. Ryan's hand reflexively reached for the rail, but Norris slapped it away before it could clamp like a vise to its false comfort.

"Use the rails, but we don't stop until we get down, agreed?"

Ryan nodded through residual sobs.

"Keep up," Norris said, smiling.

Their descent was swift and without incident save for Ryan rolling his ankle when he stepped off the ladder.

Stanley Brewer confronted his son before Ryan and Norris could cross the highway. "What were you thinking?" his father asked, but Ryan felt more accused than inquired of.

Pastor Brewer caught his son's dangling wrist and prepared to drag him across the highway in front of a much more attentive congregation than the one that had shown up for morning service.

Ryan searched the faces across the highway, scattered in the church parking lot. He had squandered his first Sunday. First impressions with all the adults who might deem his actions honorable and his character upright, irretrievably undone. He was soiled goods in fine dress to them. A whitewashed tomb.

He glanced over his shoulder to Norris, who stood dirty and gleeful near the base of the steel container he had just conquered. Norris smiled at Ryan before a rightfully distraught Mrs. Elderberry grabbed a healthy handful of Norris's grimy locks. Ryan smiled back, happy in spite of everything. He had gained something he hadn't anticipated on his first Sunday—a friend.

Solomons Foundry

I crushed peanut shells beneath my worn sneakers with each step. Flurries of houseflies narrowly escaped destruction by sole. They returned to their feast once my feet vacated their space. I followed my father down the concrete grandstand toward "good seats." Even though he was two steps ahead of me, my eyes were level with his sweating back. The sun had gone, but the heat of day remained. I wiped my brow and caught my first careful view of the grounds.

Fog veiled the pond in the center of the field. The fountain spewing from the center of the pond stirred the air but the fog persisted over the cool water. A jumbotron flashed odd names, times, and photos in a continuous montage from its massive screen, throwing a myriad of colors on the dewed grass and freshly watered track. The stadium lights washed out what would have been the jumbotron's domineering display. Clouds of moths and flies frenzied around the stadium bulbs, cycling from darkness to light.

A calloused hand gripped mine and tugged. "Come on. Can't waste your first Futurity day staring at those lights."

I followed my father's scuffed leather shoes and frayed khaki cuffs, watching my loosely tied shoelaces alternate colors on the steps in front of me. Gray. Black. Gray. Black. Gray.

A sharp voice blasted through the public address system and echoed over the grounds. The voice rattled through a spiel and announced upcoming events and races, including a dachshund sprint, the idea of which I found humorous. His words were obscured by my attention to varying tobacco scents and eager voices above me.

An endless stream of cowboy boots clapped the steps next to me. I knew without looking at their faces who they were. Sporadic steps and grunts were the old men struggling to climb or descend. Sure, pounding stomps were young men on a mission. The light rhythmic tap of roper heels, followed by small feet and sweet voices were the queens of the track and their broods. And just occasionally a pair of freshly shined Italian leather loafers glided past on their way to air conditioning.

The soft drink I had forgotten in my hand became slick in the humid air. I worried I would soon be the cause of soiled boots and soaked denim. My father, unable to pay the monetary price for such an infraction, would bear it in shame. He pulled me to the right of traffic into a sparsely occupied row much to my tiring grip's relief. I set the drink on the concrete between my feet, pulled down the retractable seat at my back. I hopped in against the seat that had been heated and softened by the sun hard plastic. I sat swinging my sneakers around my cup below.

"What do you think so far?" Dad asked. He smiled past his dense gray-striped mustache and squinted wrinkles around his eyes.

"Is it always this loud?"

Dad chuckled. "No, it's the Futurity tonight. It's the only night the perfume masks the ammonia and the voices drown out the neighs." His eyes shifted past me, finding an old friend. He smirked and waved.

"Can we get someone to drown out the voices?" I asked.

He laughed with the abandonment of care and worry that adults usually laugh when surprised by the logic of children. I hauled my soft drink into my lap while wondering what he found so funny. Now soaked in great running droplets, the outside of the cup threatened to slide through my weak grip yet again. I sat the base on the seat between my legs after each sip. The condensation soaked my tattered jeans, giving me momentary relief from the heat of the seat that cooked the underside of my thighs. My soda was cool but bordering on tepid. I lifted the lid to see where the ice had gone and found only small pieces floating in a thin layer of water above the soda. To my disappointment, we were a ten minute walk from the nearest concession and it would have seemed ridiculous to ask for more ice. I drew out the soda in massive gulps while it was still cool.

Answering my request for something to drown out the crowd was the most unwelcome surprise of the announcer's shrill voice racing to the end of his script. He welcomed the audience and sped through short advertisements for ranches, realty, and refreshments—the kind containing alcohol.

Dad tapped me on the shoulder. "Want to hold a little wager?" he asked.

"What's that?" I asked, confused and intrigued.

"It's a bet."

I was hopelessly ignorant. "And, what's that?" I asked.

"Do you remember what Mom says when I talk about quitting my job for something different?"

"Of course. "Bet you ten dollars you won't quit your job."

"That's a bet. If I don't quit, I have to give her ten dollars. If I do, she has to give me ten dollars."

It was simple, but there was something that confused me. "How come you never pay Momma that ten dollars?"

"Because I don't get paid enough to keep giving her a ten dollar bill."

"Why don't you quit and make her pay you the ten dollars?"

The light and life left his eyes for a moment. "Then I won't be able to give her the ten dollars to pay me with." The moment passed abruptly and he emerged from his solemn state. "Here's the wager. We each pick a horse and the horse that finishes first decides the winner."

I was eager for competition. Accustomed to, but uninterested in, physical challenges, a game of wisdom and intuition gave me fresh zeal. "What do I get if I win?" I asked.

"Already planning victory, huh?" He scratched the stubble on his chin and the thinning hair beneath his beret. "Whoever wins gets to control the radio on the drive home and they pick the convenience store we stop at for dinner."

"How do I choose?" I squealed.

Dad pointed to the jumbotron. "Choose your favorite."

A concise race program with ten names and their colors was displayed on screen. I could read six of them. The rest Dad had to explain to me, but I still couldn't choose my favorite. I needed to *see* my horse.

"Where are the pictures?"

Dad scanned the screen and gazed down the track. The first horses were nearing the gate. "They'll video the horses when the gate crew taxi them into the gate. You choose your horse then. We got here too late to see them parade down the track."

I waited, anxiously staring at the massive screen, excited to pick my horse, but worried I would choose poorly.

Do I choose by color? The one that looks the strongest? The calmest? The most confident looking?

Names and video streamed across the screen before I could determine the qualities that were most important and, in my mind, that a Futurity winner must possess. The first two horses entered the gate without piquing my interest. Dad called them fillies and bays, whatever that meant.

A splotchy gray gelding, according to Dad, stomped toward the third post, sauntering his hind quarters against the taxi horse. His personality was on full display. More playful than prepared. More dreamy than determined. Though I was naturally drawn to his build and obvious athleticism, I still had not found my horse.

I slouched deep into the griddle of my seat and crossed my arms. I stopped my feet from swinging and took a sour swig of my soda. Warm and flat. I scrunched my face, smacked, and set the cup on the concrete below.

Dad never looked at me, but he knew my normal countenance and gestures well. "Unfurl your lip, son. Your horse is somewhere in there. You'll know it when you see it. We tend to pick the ones most like us."

His words did little to give me hope. Discouraged, I let my chin sink into my chest while I played with the velvety threads fringing a hole in my jeans.

The announcer startled me once more with a break in his normal cadence, rising to a louder, but still rich, timbre. He claimed the next stallion had an undefeated lifetime record and was the odds-on favorite to win the Futurity.

"The King of the Quarter, the Prince of the Prairie, *Visage!*" the announcer shouted. The majority of the grandstand roared to a life that held until all the horses were in the gate. I scooted toward the edge of my seat, taut and ready.

Dad smiled. "There he is."

"Dibs!" I screamed.

Many surrounding onlookers either laughed or stared quizzically at me. Thinking I had done wrong, I slouched once again. Heat rose in my cheeks, but no amount of embarrassment could take my admiration away from the sorrel stallion. His steps were proud and sure. With raised snout and tail, he reminded me of a horse that a victorious general would consider riding but turned down because his magnificence would cast a shadow on the general himself.

He was the first horse taxied to the gate that had shown a level of energy and aggression that was borderline tasteless, barely palatable. Visage rebelled against his taxi horse, mistrusted the gate crew, and writhed like a constrained serpent when successfully guided into the gate. His muscles rippled and fired through his shining sorrel coat like clean rain over bare red clay, rendering his appearance even more appealing to someone who appreciated an athletic build.

I imagined the amount of steaks and other foods I would need to eat for such an athletic build. My mouth moistened and I swallowed the hope of a red-meat-meal. Most horses had a better chance of nutrition than I did. Tonight, it did not matter. Visage's rage and energy filled my soda-sloshed stomach with more fuel and promise than any size or cut of steak could. "He's going to win, isn't he Daddy?" I yelled over the low roar of the stand.

"Nope."

Nope? How could he be so sure? "He's never been beat. What makes you think he'll be beat tonight?"

"He's the best, but there's a dragon-slayer in the gate tonight. Besides, he wouldn't win anyway," Dad said, flatly.

"Why?" I was befuddled. Dad's seemingly irrational statements didn't confuse me as much as they convinced me he was insane.

"He's very proud tonight."

"Horses can't be proud," I rebuked.

He shrugged. "Maybe not, but everyone is proud for him. Pride is always eventually dealt with. Usually in the most humbling way possible."

I still thought he was crazy, but his assured tone and steeled resolve unsettled my own confidence—only momentarily. The cameras continued their live feed of Visage in his post while a small corner of the screen was dedicated to the following five horses. The last horse graced the larger screen not due to his status as a runner or a brilliant appearance, but thanks to the end of the camera's love affair with Visage.

The last horse, a kettle-black stallion, strode indifferently into the gate without so much as a toss of his tail. His head hung level with his back, looking less enthused than the horse taxiing him to the gate. He was passed without incident from his taxi horse to the relieved gate crew, who looked on their companion worryingly in the fourth post.

"Dragon-slayer," Dad muttered.

"Nuh-uh! That horse looks sad to be here. He looks like Uri when he was a puppy and got caught peeing in the living room."

"He's not sad."

"How do you know?"

Before he could answer, the bell and break brought the keen congregation to their feet blocking my view of the gate and runners. I turned my eyes to the grainy jumbotron while hurriedly standing on the seat. I unknowingly kicked my soft drink over, spilling it down to the row below into the main compartment of a leather purse.

Visage broke, a crazed inmate attempting to flee his captors and trip any cellmate near to ensure his escape. He thrashed between the three and five post starters. Their jockeys guided them away from the bad company, but Visage pursued the inside runners and compressed them into a tight group against the rail. His jockey attempted to gain control and refocus his stallion on the line ahead, but Visage had unfettered and indiscriminate vengeance to exact. He continued to nudge and aggravate the gray and two bays.

The first post jockey didn't allow his horse to let off and be bullied. He bravely stared down the ever-decreasing gap between his horse and the rail and leaned into the pressure from the outside. Caught in a game of equestrian pinball, the two and three post horses bumped outside with equal but opposite force. The gray, irritated and panicked, ran away from the inside and straight into Visage with more force than a casual bump.

Visage cantered away with melodramatic flair, throwing his rider, tossing his head, and throwing a fit. Who could blame him? He was only three.

There goes my control of the radio. But I was dreaming about that gas station onion burger. It oozed with a "special sauce," grease, and mushroom.

Dashed hopes brought the tunes of Dad's favorite country station to my ears and the ashy taste of burnt chicken livers to my tongue. Oblivious to the other runners and pandemonium around me, I gazed forlornly at that proud sorrel bobbing his head and throwing muddy clumps in the direction of his fallen rider. Maybe a horse could be proud, but no prouder than I was of him before the race. It had only taken me a few moments to fall in love with the view. A few moments later that view was clouded and spoiled by a fitful storm in the first hundred yards of track.

My desire had left me like the breath from the crowd. A wager made with no past experience, against an avid follower of the sport, was ignorance and pride at their peak. Ignorance and pride were the short breaks I took on my trip to deep but brief shame and the cowardly lambasting of those responsible for the loss of the wager—anyone but me. The shame left with my lost view of Visage, followed rapidly by a mental barrage of lambasting which was restrained in my mind but remained at arms on the tip of my tongue.

Why did Visage do that? Those horses on the inside caused this. Visage tricked me with his confidence. Dad tricked me, telling me my horse was in there somewhere, knowing I would be drawn to Visage's image. Dad tricked me so he could get the choice of radio and food!

The back of Dad's calloused hand tapped my feeble chest. "Take a look."

The other runners were approaching the line rapidly. The inside group had been jumbled and thrown off by the antics in the opening one hundred yards. They were beyond salvaging and had faded back beyond any hope of running in the money.

The outside six raged forward like a shore-break wave, gathering force to crash against the shoreline. The jockeys worked mightily, using their crops to great effect. The horses, guided by the riders, thrived on the energy the crowd produced. All but one.

The kettle-black stallion in violet and white colors ran his own race on the outside. He ran without need of crop or crowd. His rider, merely joining in the horse's joy, did not guide him. The stallion smoothly drove ahead of the wave and was left alone to enjoy a clean run.

He's not sad.

His competitive eyes constantly shifted from left to right, worried. His lead, barely a half-length fifty yards ago, stretched into a length and a half with more track to go.

I instinctively grabbed and squeezed the back of my Dad's soaked plaid shirt, wringing liquid over my white knuckles. My shame, anger, envy, even surprise, were forgotten. They were at the other end of the track with the visage I no longer wished to see. What remained was a newfound joy and happiness for watching a race well run, and a love of hungry, faithful hooves persevering to

the end, steadfast, running as if determined to win. His rivals and
their jockeys watched his daring performance in awe.

"You can't win a race staring at another set of hindquarters,"
Dad muttered under bated breath.

Our seats, located just beyond the finish line, shook with the
first quakes of an all-out finish. The line behind the black stallion
challenged the leader, but could not muster legs as longsuffering or
a heart with as much zeal.

The stallion crossed with momentum. His jockey struggled
to slow him even one hundred yards past the line. Hats peppered
the air, flying from those who had cheered for Visage only moments earlier. Hugs were given out freely. The smell of spilled beer
washed over the grandstand with the first stir of night air. Dad
turned to me with an open palm. "Wasn't that great?"

"Yes!" I screamed and slapped his palm. He caught my hand,
jerked me forward, and hugged me firmly, swinging me side to
side. My dangling legs knocked off a cowboy hat from a head or
two before he set me back in the row, placed a laborer's hand on my
head and smeared my hair into a curly mess. I proudly wore that
mess as my crown—a prince of my father.

❀

The parking lot was raucous and dangerous. We dodged lifted
trucks and sports cars all the way to Dad's unreliable farm truck.
Relieved to make it through the parking lot alive, but burning with
curiosity, I allowed myself a deep breath and asked, "How did you
know?"

"Know what?" Dad responded nonchalantly.

"How did you know the black one would win?" I asked.

"His name is Solomons Foundry. You might say I didn't know
for sure. I let what little wisdom I have work properly. There were
hundreds in that stadium that knew what I know. They still put
their money on Visage. That's the difference between knowledge
and wisdom. Knowledge may know stats, records, and percentages,

but wisdom discerns in such a way as to avoid the foolishness of the knowledgeable."

"Wait, why didn't you bet all the money you had on Solomons Foundry?"

He laughed at me with equal amusement as he had before. "Oh son, I'm much too wise for that."

A Fair Longing

A group of servers and one cook huddled around the television mounted over a once used fireplace. Carved wood figurines of a mariachi band stood among a garden of clay cacti on the mantle below the screen, unaware of the grave danger of being knocked off their perch by the cook's towel, which he swung wildly with each out the Dodgers got in game six of the World Series.

Aaron watched the game from his table for two in the corner next to the kitchen, as he had on most Saturdays for the past twenty-three years. He kept his table through three owners, two remodels, and a period of shutdown when Benji, the second owner, contemplated retirement. Benji had been Aaron's favorite owner. He had reinstituted the free queso and salsa before the ordering of entrees at Aaron's suggestion. Aaron considered him a dear enough friend to attend his funeral a few years back. Benji's son, Junior, managed the restaurant now, and with a style much unlike his father's, approached each table with great caution so as not to catch customers off guard and spoil their meal.

Junior shuffled into Aaron's visual range, standing next to the baseball fans, and waited for Aaron to chew and swallow a mouthful of *bistec ranchero* before asking "How's the plate today, Mr. Aaron?"

Aaron took a quick slurp of his margarita from its polystyrene cup—a vessel choice he had picked up from Benji to avoid the worried glances of his Baptist brothers and sisters—and answered, "Not too shabby. Seasoning on the steak was spot on tonight."

"Wonderful. You enjoying the game as well? I can't seem to keep my employees away from it," Junior said, raising his voice loud enough for the baseball lovers to hear.

The servers scattered off to their stations, trying to appear busy on the sluggish October night. The lone cook, a balding pudgy-faced man with rosy cheeks, turned and rolled his eyes so dramatically at Junior that his thick black unibrow disappeared under his Dodger-themed bandana. The cook slapped his towel over his shoulder like a shovel and tottered back to the kitchen, returning to the prairie cook's equivalent of digging a ditch.

Junior qualified his cook's behavior. "Chino is still upset that I have yet to replace the TV we used to have in the kitchen. I would gladly replace it for them, but he refuses to quit throwing knives at the screen when the Dodgers lose."

Aaron chuckled. "I'll pay for the TV myself if he keeps making plates like this. Danny and I used to wager his mother's appetizers over each pitch. I gained a lot of weight during his early years."

Both men laughed and Junior, looking more jovial and less serious, took the seat across from Aaron. "How is Daniel? I have not seen him or Tanya since we graduated."

"He's been living a grand life in Montana. They have two kids now and he makes a killing peddling this stuff," Aaron said, lifting a fork full of steak.

"Beef? He always said he wouldn't go into the cattle industry. It's funny where the natural course of events will take a man. I swore off *Mama Guapa* when I was waiting tables one night and now I'm running the place." Junior leaned forward and whispered, "And I actually like it!"

They laughed once more and spoke of school memories Danny and Junior shared. The conversation gave Aaron great heartache. He disliked the practice of reminiscing to pass the time or to heal wounds when he found, in his own experience, memories often widened wounds. He preferred the more impersonal nostalgia centered around times he'd never experienced himself, or the age-old debate over who was the greatest baseball player of all time. Anything to distract him from memories the people of prairie culture continually conjured up out of habit. It was their preference over any political or spiritual talk, which usually came up when they ran out of memories.

Junior returned to his responsibilities after what Aaron considered an appropriate amount of reminiscing, brief, even for a curt man such as himself. One of the servers, Junior's young cousin, brought a fresh polystyrene-cloaked margarita after she had heard him slurping the last tidbits from the other cup. She hurriedly set it down, nearly tipping it over, and scurried back to the huddle that reconvened below the screen as soon as Junior had returned to the kitchen.

While Aaron and Junior had been talking, the Dodgers manager had replaced their cruising left-handed starter with a hard-throwing, right-handed middle reliever without a viable off-speed pitch. The manager's decision saw his two-to-nothing lead slip into a two-to-two tie leaving the heart of the Astros dugout slobbering for more runs in their no-outs, bases-loaded situation. "Bone-head," Aaron said when the cameras found the Dodgers manager sulking in the lonesome end of the dugout. His players, unwilling to peer at their dejected leader, watched dumbly as their calamity worsened.

Aaron finished the steak and left most of his cilantro rice untouched. The waitress had set his check conveniently next to his margarita without his notice. He grabbed the check – and his margarita, to go – and headed for the front counter to pay. He would need to let Junior know the waitress accidentally left off his second margarita. He paused in front of the screen to watch the Astros tally three more runs, thanks to a base-clearing double from their Rookie of the Year candidate. The *Mama Guapa* employees, every one a Dodger loyalist, groaned collectively. Chino, who had miraculously re-appeared under the screen, pulled down on his rosy cheeks, straining his already fajita-irritated eye sockets. He cursed vehemently in Spanish into his towel. Aaron suspected he had more than hopes and dreams wagered on the series.

"Give it up folks. Astros in six," Aaron muttered behind them before continuing to the front desk to pay. Aaron took a peppermint-flavored toothpick from a box near the register, inserted it into the corner of his mouth, and thought of taking one of the complimentary candies before handing Junior the check behind the counter. "Make sure you put two margaritas on that check and teach your cousin how to count," Aaron said.

Junior didn't look up from the check as he added up the charges on an ancient cash register. "She counts well already. I taught her one margarita for you and one margarita for us. I'm a great teacher."

Charity gave Aaron feelings of uneasiness, thinking he was receiving unwarranted pity. He protested firmly as a father does to a son in a moment of the son's folly. "No, I need to pay, Junior. Your daddy always let me pay."

Junior, aware of Aaron's individualistic pride, stared with blank eyes and a well-leveled lip at his father's old, white, and flaxen-haired friend and said, "You have already paid for one drink, Mr. Aaron. You have bartered with your memories for the other. Thank you for the conversation."

Aaron did indeed feel as if he had paid for the conversation with his nerves, and no amount of margaritas could measure equally across the scales in payment for grief that an allusion to the past can occasionally produce. He worked the peppermint toothpick over his teeth, using his lips to pass the tool from corner to corner, the wood clicking subtly against each tooth. There was no one there to remove it from his mouth out of annoyance from his habit. There was no one there to shove him out the door because his friendly conversation was causing Junior to neglect his responsibilities. In his most recent days, Aaron was forced to see himself out.

"I enjoyed it and I'll be back next week for another one, Mr. Rocha," Aaron said.

Junior, realizing that the use of his last name was meant to signify the transfer of respect from his father's legacy to him, grinned so forcibly that Aaron worried the young man would crack his pale, chapped lips. The young owner's first expression of an emotion other than seriousness reminded Aaron very much of Benji.

Junior tried to respond in full voice, but could only manage a broken whisper that carried all the gratitude and respect he wished to convey. "Thank you, Mr. Aaron. Adiós."

⤫

The walk home from *Mama Guapa* seemed a block longer for his feet each trip, and his lungs would have agreed. With shortened days, darkness rushed across the prairie with haste, but thanks to well-lit streets, Aaron could see each crack in the concrete sidewalk, each one an obstacle for his aged and shallow steps. His left knee locked on occasion due to internal scarring and a weak right hip, caused, no doubt, by his baseball days. His creaky frame dragged his leg with a limpness that worsened each week.

Most of the houses on his three-block walk neared their centennial era. Tapered brick pillars guarded their vast front porches, but many, having been restored with new flooring and lighting, invited any who passed on the sidewalk to come and rest a spell. Their glowing entrances stood in purposeful contrast to the cold light of the street. Familial sounds from within beckoned to all whose souls were parched like the prairie dust, which whipped up out of fields from afar and glided across the street. Though unseen, the wind used the dust to make its whims known, covering cars and clothing, reminding men of its presence and to where they would return.

Aaron heard the familiar sounds of excitable baseball commentary coming from one home in particular. Its brick had been painted a pale green. During the winter the color was too vibrant and in the summer too dull, but at night tangerine lights affected Aaron's senses so profoundly that he envied the owner's lit and lively home, even before he noticed the man did not enjoy the game alone. There was a life there that he missed dearly. He rolled the toothpick across his teeth once more and he heard no protest.

Aaron continued walking until he reached the original stone steps and porch of his own home. The pillars still encased the old heavy-duty bug screens which had collected large tape-patched tears over the years. He could no longer find bug screens of the correct size or durability in any of his yearly catalogs, and he refused to settle for less than the quality of those bygone years. He unlocked his front door in darkness. The struggle with the locks took a breath or two from him, and as the door swung open he inhaled the cellar-like air of his home. There was no one there to bemoan him not using the light switch next to the door. There was no one there to hear him respond with, "We used to never have to lock the door anyway."

After a shuffle inside and a deliberate effort to push pesky memories aside, Aaron flicked a switch next to the door and dim incandescent bulbs revealed stereotypical southwestern decor. He took three sluggardly steps to his left, set his margarita on a rickety end table with a built-in lamp, and eased into a birch wood rocking chair covered in colorful wool saddle blankets. He absently rolled the toothpick across his teeth once more, without a protest from anyone. He sucked the moistened peppermint resin from the toothpick over his tongue with an irksome smack. No one came to pull the pick from his teeth's grip and demand he finally learn some manners.

He turned on the television that Danny had helped him mount to the brick wall a few years back. He switched over to the World Series coverage, which had morphed into an Astros celebration. "Told ya," he said and looked over to an empty matching birch wood chair. Disenchanted with the fulfillment of his prophecy, he turned off the television.

He ached and popped his joints through his nightly hygiene routine. He found a set of flannel pajamas to protect him from the stark drop in nighttime temperature. No one was there to chastise him for neglecting to reignite the wood burning stove at the heart of the home.

Aaron slipped under the heavy covers of his bed and rolled to face the wall on his side of the bed, the toothpick pressed against the inside of his cheek, pinching the inside of his mouth and gums. He winced and worked it across his teeth to the other corner.

Suddenly he spat out the toothpick. The tiny birch utensil clicked a few times on the floor, rolled, and eventually stopped somewhere in the darkness. He rotated and said to the empty side of the bed, "I know. I forgot to brush my teeth." The only reply was from the wind, which had found the gaps of the bug screen and crooks of the tree branches to whistle through.

The effort of standing from his prone position winded him. He limped back into his bathroom, the pain in his hip nearly parallel to the pain at his core. The wood panels beneath his feet groaned and popped along with his joints until their sounds were indistinguishable. Arid prairie static magnetized his pajamas to his skin and tingled everywhere they touched him. Unable to itch away all points of sensation, he targeted the most bothersome and rubbed them away, saddened there was not another pair of hands to help him. He brushed his teeth and returned to the lukewarm dent he had left in the sheets. He sat there, reluctant to lay down next to the empty pillow.

Without a face to adore across what lately seemed to be an endless expanse of bed, Aaron instead watched the shadows cast by his neighbor's streetlight through the pecans as they waved their wretched hands over the thin teal curtains in his room. Their motion threatened to rock his eyes to sleep, but they could do no such courtesy for his soul.

Aaron whispered haltingly into the dark, "She would have replaced the toothpick with her lips."

He let his left shoulder slap against the spring mattress with a lax thud and from his back he laughed until his dinner caused him a tightening discomfort in his bowels. "She would have been upset about that order of extra onions, though."

Aaron, aware he reeked more of loneliness than of onions, fell asleep wondering if, within himself, there existed a strength sufficient enough to carry on in contentedness.

Breathing Love Back to Life

Barefoot and braising veal, Constance leaned over the stew. Hands on hips and pursed lips, she concentrated on the second course cooking in her father's iron skillet he had wrapped in used kitchen cloth for a wedding gift. Her parents had nothing more to give when she and Virgil were married. Her eyes welled with tears each time she blindly gripped the twisted iron handle from the cabinet, too tall for her vision. She lifted her pinstripe apron to her nose and blew out sorrow.

"Onion and cayenne pepper get me every time," she said. Her voice quivered, but never cracked.

Virgil stopped prepping vegetables next to her and stared at his wife's figure. She pretended not to notice, keeping busy with a ladle and the array of spices at her disposal. She whiffed scents across her face, enjoying the steam and sweat that accompany extreme focus over a cooking meal.

"Stop staring, Virg. I want to make this meal perfect. I can't do that with you staring," she grumbled.

Virgil laughed, returned to prepping the vegetables, and said, "I'm a man, Connie. If a man wants to admire his *one* while she works, let him admire his *One.*"

She ignored what she liked to call his "goofy sentiments." Her hands floated just out of range of scalding heat. She was mission bound, but she still had enough time for a smirk and shake of her head. The adoration had always been mutual, but she doubted he would enjoy her form when her hair and hands had seen many more vintages than the wine they could afford. She felt his eyes, but wanted his touch more.

"I forgot the cumin! Nate . . ."

Their son's name hadn't been uttered in such a natural way since his death. She had to force his name from her lips, but never his memory to her mind. Whether the oncoming presence of their son's estranged fiancé or the cooking of his favorite meal had conjured his name, Constance knew not but slowly collapsed to her knees. She gasped and fought desperately to hold in a mournful moan before lying on the sun-bleached linoleum, curled into a tender ball of sorrow on the floor. She held the ladle near her nose, letting the golden brown broth drip into her splayed graying hair on the floor—the first coloring it had had in years.

Constance vaguely noticed the familiar click of the gas stove's heat being reduced to a warming simmer. Virgil knelt near his wife, his Marine-issued joints popping and cracking. He gently cupped her head under one palm and gripped her belly with the other. He didn't speak, knowing his lips were best used by lightly kissing her neck and breathing on her numbed skin. He called it, "Breathing Love back to life."

Disgusted with her grief and still mournful disposition, she attempted to struggle away from Virgil's grip, but was quickly reminded how easily a gifted machine gunner could hold fast to his best friend.

"Don't move, Momma," he whispered.

"Virg, we need to finish cooking before she gets here. I want her to sit down to a warm and ready plate," Constance whined, but didn't struggle from his masculine grip. She nestled her cheek into his palm and pressed his fingers into her lips. She constantly longed for the rest she found in prayers and in his hands, enjoying it now more than ever.

Virgil continued to breathe on and kiss the nape of her neck. He hummed a tune against her skin and rubbed her cheek and belly with his thumbs.

The storm that had been clouding Constance's mind and heart gradually calmed. She listened to Virgil's humming, recognized it, but couldn't name it. "What song is that?" she asked.

"It's an oldie. Care to guess? It's from before our courtship."

She sighed. "Just tell me. I'm not in the thinking mood."

His lips smiled against her skin and he kissed her. "I whistled it to you when I would walk into the office from the lumberyard. It's from—"

Constance placed her worn feet on cabinets in need of a sand and stain and pressed her back deep into Virgil's chest. "*Red Is the Rose*," she whispered with reminiscent pleasure.

"You remembered," his voice rumbled against her. "Would you like me to sing it for you while we cook?"

Her eyes welled with joyous tears, but she dared not release them. She nodded. She would love nothing more than his voice filling the space where her thoughts and memories roamed dangerously free. She reveled in the times when they were newlyweds, eating thin, and thinly dressed. They were given to much love and meager money.

Virgil sang and prepped. Constance cooked and tasted. They practiced their perfected routine and drew each meal from memory, reaching reflexively for spice or sauce. Working with the background of Virgil's aging voice lowered Constance's anxiousness and forced her to enjoy the cooking she was determined to struggle through. She loved her labors. She enjoyed the feeling of falsely purging sorrows through sweat, until they inevitably returned with the washing of dishes, where Nate should be at the end of their assembly line, cheerfully drying and stacking.

Working in a kitchen fit for three, but with only two, reminded Constance of trying on her maternity clothes years after Nate's birth. There was space that needed filling.

Does Virgil feel awkward, too?

She knew it was futile to entertain the thought because Virgil didn't have to feel the same—in fact, he rarely felt the same as her—but she didn't like loneliness in her emotions. She wanted him to at least know how she felt and she didn't know how to bring it up without stumbling into the dark chasm that was sorrow for her son.

"Would you ever think about getting a smaller place, Virg?" Constance asked.

The rapid click of knife's edge against bamboo board halted. She heard Virgil's long and bony shoulders shrug meditatively under his shirt. "Maybe," Virgil answered. She didn't really want a new place for any practical reason, but knew it would be best to appeal to Virgil's love of practicality and frugalness.

The harsh sound of chopping returned with more irregular frequency, betraying his preoccupation. Then the chopping halted again. "Why a smaller place? This place already seems small to me."

"We can't fill this place together. We won't use most of this space and someone else could really use this. I want to really fill a place, you know?"

"That just means we need to invite more people over for dinner. Have I told you I've thought about inviting the old gang back over for coffee in the mornings?"

Constance whipped her head around to glare at him with anticipatory indignation. "If you invite the Gallagher twins over for coffee ever again, I'll ring you out and hang your skinny ass over the line. They don't understand that coffee starts after nine in the morning and not five. The sun must be up to drink coffee in *my* world."

"You mean you'll only wring me out *once* for inviting them?" he asked playfully.

"I mean it, Virg!"

"Okay, my One. Coffee and confrontation is a terrible combination. I'll get them over at ten. They don't show up for anything less than a plate of donuts, though," Virgil said, hopefully.

Constance worked silently, avoiding Virgil's leading comments. She wouldn't mind company, even those twin irritants, two jackrabbits that listened to and hopped between conversations as if anyone wanted to hear their opinion. More people would bring more happiness, conversation, and intimacy, but it could not bring the joy she fought so strongly to grasp.

Constance stirred and smelled the braised veal.

Almost done.

She plated the asparagus and her spiced new potatoes next to a creamy mushroom sauce meant for the incoming veal. She hadn't made the dish in years. Worry about Virgil and Ruth's receptiveness to the meal caused Constance to sweat more than her normal cooking sweat. She wiped her brow and upper lip with the back of her oven mitt that she used to grip the iron skillet.

"Virg, could you please uncork the wine. It needs to breathe for a moment before Ruth gets here."

Before the cork squeaked twice the doorbell rang to the tune of Handel's *Messiah*. Constance groaned. "She's already here! And can we change the doorbell, please?"

Virgil popped the cork and handed the bottle to Constance. "Yes, love. I'll go let her in." He kissed her forehead and shuffled to the door in his insulated house shoes.

Constance stepped into the dining room and smelled the cork Virgil had laid on her mother's handmade tablecloth, leaving another stain. She remembered all the stains like monuments to the many meals they had enjoyed or loathed together.

The click of the lock and scrape of door against frame preceded the formal rural greeting of audible joy and familiarity. Ruth's sweet voice softened Constance's anxious and stony heart toward a meal she anticipated to suffer through. She now couldn't wait to see the woman whom her son loved and who loved him back. She missed watching their interactions no matter how much she feared the loss of his love to her. She experienced the wealth of not just his love, but Ruth's as well.

"Come on in and fill your plate," Virgil exclaimed and then lowered his voice, "We don't want Connie thinking more of herself than she ought, but I'm sure this is her best veal yet."

Ruth giggled with all the sincerity and adorableness Constance had always known her to have. The same giggle she had received from the grass-stained and muddy-footed little girl who would sneak in the back door of the house for a whiff of dinner.

A woman, a potential wife to be enjoyed in her blessed youth, stepped into the soft, dull light of an antique chandelier. Her chin was tilted down, dark eyes locked on the hostess through thick natural eyelashes. "Mrs. Stern, please forgive me, I'm late. I had to help Mom prepare for the potluck."

Constance said nothing. She scurried over to Ruth and embraced her tightly, lifting her from the floor and squeezing the breath from her lungs. "We've missed you," Constance said, still hugging the daughter-in-law she wished she had had.

"Easy, my love," Virgil warned his wife, fearing Ruth would soon faint.

Constance released Ruth. "I missed you guys, too." Ruth narrowly avoided crying through her sentence.

Fearful of tears himself, Virgil directed the attention back to the meal. "Ruth gets first choice of the meat as the guest," he chuckled and looked down thoughtfully, "It's been a long time since I've had the chance to say that."

Constance smiled at Ruth's radiance and pecan-colored hair. "She was more girl then. And now, she's all woman."

Ruth blushed and said, "I don't feel like it. I still find myself wanting to stop the car and go play whenever I see other girls on a soccer field."

Virgil shook his head and grimaced. "I never understood why you loved soccer so much. You were a track star in the making. Nate was pretty quick and you outran him all the way up until . . ."

The name and memories oppressed them. They knew he would have to become the subject of the dinner conversation, but now, in this moment that they expected to rekindle relationship over anything other than a mutual love and sorrow for one who was dead, was much too early. Ruth saved the conversation well. "In the sport of track, or any racing for that matter, there is only one chance to celebrate. In soccer there are usually three or four chances to celebrate. I played for the celebration." She giggled, seeing Virgil's face contort worse than before and knowing he used to cheer her on with more zeal than anyone else in the stands.

They all sat with their meals and began to enjoy melted veal fat and buttery asparagus. It didn't take Constance long to let her fork rattle to a stop on her plate and ask, "So Ruth, what is the area of study these days?"

"Shouldn't we let her eat more than one bite before we make her talk about school, love?" Virgil asked.

"No! I've been wanting to talk about this since I agreed to dinner," Ruth protested. "I believe Mrs. Connie will like it."

"Delay no further!"

"Black bears!" Ruth's eyes sparkled like opals in a jewelry store when the lights in the display cabinets were turned on.

Constance, unable to withhold her obvious happiness, held her hands wide, gesturing to all the bear figurines and paintings that adorned her shelves and walls. "Like all these! I love this news. Did you hear that, Virg?"

Virgil dropped his face into his open palms and muttered through them. "Oh, brother."

"Are you not excited for Ruth?" she asked, playfully.

"You know I am. I'm just worried about the quality of conversation dropping to an all-time low." He groaned and added, "I think I'd rather talk about soccer before bears."

With his fears confirmed about the quality of conversation, Virgil polished off the wine bottle on his own while his wife, too entrenched in engaging and fruitful conversation to care about the polka dot pattern he was spilling onto her mother's tablecloth, spoke with the now woman she still saw as her daughter-in-law. Constance secretly imagined that Ruth truly was their daughter-in-law and would continue visiting them in the future with more stories of bears, wildlife, and open country that Constance would likely never see.

Eager to steer clear of bears, Virgil made an effort to make Ruth the focal point of conversation. "Sounds like you got a lot figured out, little sister. When do you graduate and what are the plans for after that? You can't chase bears your whole life."

Ruth giggled, but expressed a hidden solemnity with forlorn eyes and slack lips. "Well, the future is one of the reasons I came here. Being at school for so long and keeping my head in books, I don't feel as if I've been able to truly move forward with a future.

"I haven't had many connections through studies and research, and I've never been the best at making new friends. You guys know I've had the same three friends since I was six, but I've been able to get out and connect for the first time since . . ."

Ruth held back unhinged sorrow that, if released, could plunge her back into the depths of self-isolation from which she was speaking. Virgil and Constance looked on—both harboring true sympathy for Ruth and a hopeful expectancy for her conclusion.

"I'm sorry," Ruth muttered. She hurriedly wiped away tears with quivering hands. "The point is I have opened up, partially thanks to you two. I know I haven't been around much, but your emails and letters were part of the few early sweet spots in my life and have become more delightful and treasured ever since. You kept me tethered to a yearning for relationship and a hope that it would come, something I have come to understand as a built-in need for us all. I wanted to express my appreciation in person."

Constance reached out diagonally toward Ruth's hand. Ruth gripped it like it was the last dessert left at the table. Constance squeezed her hand in solidarity. "We love you, Ruth."

Still crying and wiping tears with her free hand, Ruth said, "I know. You've shown me love ever since you met me and you proved it best in the hardest times. I'll always be grateful for that."

Constance tapped Ruth's hand with her fingers. "And, we'll still be here to show it from now on."

Virgil raised his glass. "Here. Here."

"I know, but I won't be here and likely won't see this place ever again. You see, through the recent connections I've been able to make through school and researching, oddly enough . . ." Her voice quavered. "I've been able to meet someone."

No longer held to each other by a mutual sorrow and hope for what had passed, Constance removed her hand from Ruth's grip.

Ruth continued, "I met him through studying the correlation of fenced ranches and male black bear territorial patterns.

His name is Tim. He's a Montana game warden. He's asked me to marry him."

Constance simultaneously felt the weight of undeclared jealousy for herself and relief for Ruth. Virgil sat up from his vino-induced slouch and said, "Go on. Tell us more! What kind of pistol does he get to carry?"

Encouraged by Virgil's interest and dearly hoping for Constance's, Ruth smiled through her tears as her words spilled out. "He's quiet and kind, even though his arms and shoulders would make most grizzlies think twice before challenging him to a fight. He played baseball for Oregon State before he graduated and decided he wanted to be a game warden. He's very upright in his judgment, but gracious to most of the ignorant hunters. His parents own a big cattle ranch near Missoula and he has worked there his entire life. He's proven himself loyal and humble in his relationships. He's really one of those rare mighty men who put themselves below others in their own thought. I watched him give an illegally shot elk to a family on one of the reservations who had just lost their father and had no income other than government assistance. He's now trying his best to mentor the two sons and daughter that the man left behind."

Constance couldn't help hearing a description of Nate from a different family and background. Their qualities and countenances matched. Their stature and natures sounded similar. But, the tell-tale sign Ruth had found a character like Nate was the clear adoration in Ruth's voice. She was not just describing a remarkable man she had heard about or wished to meet. She was telling the intimate details of a life she longed to join with her own.

"Surely, you told him yes, didn't you?" Constance interrupted—more to gather the information she wished untrue than to hope for Ruth's affirmation.

"Of course! I didn't wear my ring here so I wouldn't give myself away too quickly, but I said yes even before he opened the box and I saw the ring. It's back at Mama's. I'll send you an email with pictures of it. It looks much better when it's off my man hands, but you need to see it with the Rocky mountains as a backdrop. It's like the diamond was meant to be there."

Constance remembered that she still had the receipt for the ring that Nate had bought for Ruth in her armoire.

"His mother is like you, Mrs. Connie. She can't cook as good as you, but she's warm, inviting, caring, and it is no wonder Tim turned out to be so kind and protective."

Constance suddenly despised the fact that anyone else could hold all those qualities as she had and wished that somehow she could monopolize them for herself.

"His dad is more of a rancher than a sports fanatic, but I think you'd like him anyway, Mr. Stern. He's very knowledgeable about baseball."

"Does he hunt like Tim?" Virgil asked, hopefully.

"No, his work keeps him from hunting, and frankly, so does Tim's. I don't think he's been on a hunt for three years now because they've kept him so busy during season."

"That's too bad," Constance said, more as a reflex to unfortunate news rather than a true concern for the man's hunting habits.

"You'll still come back to your mother's from time to time, won't you?" Virgil asked.

"That's the other thing. Tim has built two homes on their family land and offered to give Mama one for free. All she has to do is bake him desserts for the rest of her life." Ruth giggled. "She happily agreed once she found out there was a good heater and that Tim would keep her fireplace going all winter."

Ruth and Virgil laughed, but Constance could only force herself into a pleasant smile. She had been stabbed in her core by the original news that Ruth had found someone to replace the role of her son, but with each new divulgence the dagger seemed to be driven deeper. A woman she never met eclipsed her. A man she could only imagine as less handsome than Virgil in sullied ranch clothes, had replaced her husband's crucial role in bringing Ruth back to a place where she could leave her house and mingle at church. And now, the little family Constance had grown to love and adore, Ruth and her mother, was being whisked away to a place that Oklahoma could not match in beauty or bounty.

"Tomorrow will be our last Sunday potluck. It will be sad to leave everyone here, but we're excited and thankful for your shared excitement."

"Of course!" Virgil exclaimed. "The future is bright indeed. We do expect photos, especially when you two start having children."

"You'll get all the photos you want!"

Constance bemoaned the thought of sifting through photos she hadn't taken of grandbabies that weren't hers.

"What do you think, Mrs. Connie? Am I making the right choice or does this all seem too quick and wild?"

Desiring to affirm the movement was hurried and the prospects too good to be true, Constance instead composed her pride and answered, rightly, "I think you've been given a great gift, Ruth. If you didn't take that gift, it would be wrong and I'd be the first call to repentance you would receive."

Constance squeezed Ruth's hand for the last time. She truly wished Ruth well and would pray blessings over her for the rest of her days, but still couldn't help feeling she was the spare wheel beneath an abandoned farm truck, left to watch the work being done without her. She was there for Ruth's beginning and middle, but would be absent from the wonderful climax and ending. She felt as she had after Nate's death, stuck on the prairie without purpose or a plan.

"Thank you," Ruth said. Her tears flowed freely. "I wanted your approval above all others, Mrs. Connie."

The admission was a small consolation to Constance, who preferred her own course of events that she had manufactured in her mind for the past six years. "I'm very happy to hear that," Constance said.

The group sat in silent contentedness. All were truly happy for Ruth and her mother, but Constance could not shake her sentiments, wishing it had been her to become the girl's mother-in-law. Suddenly she yearned to be in her closet, behind Virgil's wedding suit, sobbing for what she felt had been unjustly taken from her, though she knew she had been given much more in the years she had with Nate and Ruth than had been taken from her in the years to come. Their moments with her were always rich and abundant with joy.

Ruth rubbed Constance's hand with both of her hands and stood. "I promised Mama I'd help with dessert and I bet the casserole is nearly finished, but I'm not leaving without hugs," Ruth said.

Virgil and Constance embraced her with the force that comes with deep relation and pending sorrow for the fading of that connection. Ruth threw her pea coat over her shoulders and followed Virgil to the door. Constance and Virgil watched her skip away, as she did when she was young and barefooted, down their concrete path.

The warm light from the chandelier appeared much brighter now that night had fallen on the prairie. One of the old bulbs that Virgil always mentioned replacing but never replaced flickered randomly, threatening to burn out in their presence.

The bulb, usually a source of irritation for Constance, drew no attention from her, as she dwelled between envy and hopelessness, where no light is found and darkness consumes the dweller.

Virgil slouched next to her in a creaking chair, staring at Ruth's untouched food. "It was good to see that girl," he muttered with father-like fondness.

Constance played with her stew. She filled her spoon with broth, lifted it from the bowl, and dumped it back into the bowl, repeatedly.

Virgil sensed his wife's discontent. He slipped his hand beneath the table and searched blindly until he found her warm thigh beneath her apron and dress.

"We can't do anything now. There's no work left for us," Constance said. She stared into the darkness outside their dining room window that covered their corner of town. The wind intensified, blowing dry, fallen leaves across the face of the window before her, but her empty gaze ignored them all.

"What are you talking about, love? We have more work than we can handle now," Virgil protested.

"You know what I mean."

Virgil sat up and gently rubbed his wife's thigh. "No, I don't. Your hands are full with the diner, catering, and this house. I have Dad's store to manage and the volunteering at the VA every month nearly kills us. What more work do you want? Lately I've considered telling you to slow down."

She gradually rotated her gaze toward Virgil. Pain, sorrow, and confusion replaced her emotionless expression. "I'm not talking about working for money or keeping busy. I'm talking about what I was meant for. It's gone. It skipped down the street just now. It was crushed under a semi on Highway 3. I held it in my hands, in my body, four times before it ever had a chance to enter the world living and breathing. Don't think about telling me to slow down when I never got a chance to finish what I started."

Virgil stopped rubbing her thigh and looked longingly into her eyes, calling who she used to be before all the sorrow and trial to come back. "I am sorry," he said.

"We have been over this. It's not your fault, Virg."

"No, I'm not saying sorry for all the things that have happened. I'm saying sorry for not directing you toward thankfulness. I watched, irresponsibly, as you defined yourself by Nate's death. I let you dwell in what you thought was your failure to bring a pregnancy to term. And now, it's happening, again, with Ruth. Instead of being thankful for all the times you cooked that girl a meal, all the tears you've wiped from her eyes when she thought her daddy left because she was not loveable, you crush yourself under the weight of your own plan and desires."

"I've never been able to finish one of my plans. They're all foiled before I've done them," Constance growled.

"That's because any plan we make or could make has remnants of folly. They're flawed in their beginnings. You must be thankful. We must be thankful, even when only small portions of our heart's desires are fulfilled. And, you must be thankful when they are not."

Constance shimmied her thigh away from Virgil's touch and went back to playing with her stew. Virgil rested his forehead on the stained tablecloth, despaired that he could not wrest his wife's soul away from the dark grip of discontent.

Weary and anxious, they waited in vain in the dead and still space of the dining room for something to change. Virgil fought sleep and Constance fought reason.

Virgil lifted his head with a boyish grin. Constance rolled her eyes when she glimpsed the combination of face and expression she could never resist warming toward in their early years, thinking he used it cheaply, now.

"I'm thankful for a wife, who devoted her life and energy to her husband, child, and other children that needed her. I'm thankful for work, whether to keep me busy or make money. I'm even thankful for nights like these, where I wonder if there is anything about me or my life, which you could possibly be thankful for. I'm thankful for a son . . ." Virgil fought back a baleful cry and continued, "For a dutiful son, who loved a woman that we were allowed to care for after he was gone. And I'm thankful, in this very moment, right now, for a wife who has endured it all. She has worked out her calling, carefully and reverently. She has added honor to the meaning of wife, mother, and friend. These are the things I've been given and I'm most thankful for them."

Virgil stood and walked toward their bedroom with tear-filled eyes, a set jaw, and a government-issued step. His house shoes sung with rhythmic swishes over the wood of the hallway.

Constance held tight to her filthy pride and bitterness as one might to reasoning they had just used and lost an argument with. She wore both like badges she had received at Nate's funeral from onlookers who whispered, "That poor momma," or "She's a strong woman." She never had to be told of the things that had been taken away from her over the years. She kept a running tally. When others experienced loss, she arrived first with meals, condolences, and a subtle reminder, brought by her presence, that they would now need a will at least half as strong as hers to carry on. No one, absolutely no one, in the area had experienced loss as frequently or deeply as she had, except Virgil. They were all forced to relate to something, those who had lost someone and found one of Constance's heavy casseroles and light pity, when their loved ones had died. But she had Virgil. She had his soldierly virility at her side and under her bedraggled arms when they hung low with sorrow and grief. And now, he gave thanks for a life she thought should be pitied above all. She held tight until Virgil nearly made it to their bedroom door and his thankfulness overwhelmed her. She stood, throwing her chair aside. She hustled after her husband, running for the first time since Nate's youth and persevering past an ache in her joints she had never experienced before to reach her husband.

Virgil turned in time to catch his falling wife, who trusted his machine gunner hands to protect her from the floor.

"I'm thankful," she cried. "I'm thankful."

Virgil held her close and fell rigidly into the hallway wall. He let their combined weight ease them down against the dark floral wallpaper. His rear dropped to the floor. Constance's back lay across his chest and her head rested on his bicep. Virgil leaned forward with his lips hovering above the back of her neck. He hummed *Red Is the Rose between kisses.*

Proper Pigsties

Stepping from plowed field to feral ground mystically transported Cillian to his distant future manhood that was at the same time forward and backward. He imagined a stout beard like his father's gracing his face, and fighter's hands strong enough to remove the oil filter on the tractor without cursing. Instead of a windbreaker, his brawny shoulders were wrapped in the toasty bulk of a calf-length fur coat, much like a Viking lord's winter dress, crafted of pelts taken from some ancient arctic beast in the north of Europe. His feet were shod in sturdy buckskin moccasins, cinched tightly to his calves by the animal's durable sinews, allowing him to brave a puddle or two before his size five Reeboks seeped chilled reality between his toes.

The sparsely wooded draws between fields and pastures didn't entice him away from the house as much as they represented his haven from it. He craved the taste of windblown dust coating his teeth rather than whatever his mother's competing friends had cooked. The scent of the musty undergrowth, decomposing in the sun, rather than homemade scented candles that smelled of self-aggrandizement.

He reveled in his escapes from the meetings of the "church ladies," where the only thing they treasured more than faux friendship was their reasoning for why their disobedient children struggled with the personalities of school teachers, who had similar proclivities to their own.

Cillian's mother kept his adventures local and his disobediences short-lived. She preferred the education that a farm and home brought over the government school's contribution to pliable hearts and minds, but sent him there anyway because that's what a good mother did. She sent him to the disobedient and brought him back each day to teach the valuable lesson of constant correction. But Cillian believed a man made his own corrections. He sprinted to the wild each weekend to find those corrections and conform to them.

He stomped through the crunch of cottonwood leaf piles near the banks of the only creek on the farm before he heard his mother's shrill call echo between the trees. If only he had crossed before she had summoned him! Then, he assumed, it would have been a worthy excuse to not have heard her, as if the creek acted as a barrier, a supernatural answering machine for unwanted calls.

He hated returning home, even when God called him back with the darkness. He begged within his heart for days immortal, void of the petty duties of attendance and decorum at such things as potlucks and play dates.

Viking fantasy defeated by his duty of sonship, his beard fell away, the damp windbreaker replaced his warm, dry fur coat, and soggy size fives hindered his wretched steps back to the house.

ᵍᵉᵃ

Clods of dark field loam mixed with scarlet clay fell and rolled away from Cillian's caked shoes as he stamped up the stairs and across the pine porch his father had built, leaving behind muddy footprints sprinkled with blades and seeds of disked weeds. The Frasier twins wrestled over a particular color of toy car next to his mother's wicker chairs and patio table. He loved to watch the boys interact and often wondered what joy it must be to have been born with your ever-present best friend and willing opponent. The screen door was shut, but the dark stained wood door was cracked enough for his mother's instruction to escape with the dry heat of a wood fire. "Remove those soiled shoes and brush off that denim, young man."

Cillian normally scoffed at commands, but welcomed any delay of the scrutinized entrance he had to make before the women, who still found holding other children to the standard southern etiquette but never placing their own brood under such oppression an acceptable practice. Cillian weathered their happy judgments as long as there was sweet tea and any salty snack to smack at them with.

His lack of haste was clearly unappreciated, judging by his mother's wide-eyed warning glare, complete with pursed lips. He smelled dehydrating jerky, perfect for disgusting the mothers, who refused to wipe their own children's noses.

He rushed past the pharisaical stares to the kitchen and found a plate of baby carrots, diced tomatoes, and ranch dressing. He giggled and casually dumped all but the dressing in the trash. Reaching around the dehydrator to where his mother had hidden the already dehydrated meat, he grabbed a man's handful, dropped it in the ranch, and tossed it like salad. He strutted back to the living room, smacking and licking his fingers. He hopped up onto the toasted, brick hearth extension and leaned against the edge of the lintel. Red hot coals settled in the neat pile they had been shoveled into, covered by a thin blanket of velvety ash. Cillian's feet were exposed by the holes in his socks, causing the heat of the brick to become intolerable if he left them in one place too long. He alternated the foot he stood on to continue warming without burning, a cat's slow dance on a hot tin roof, all the while gnawing and ripping pieces of jerky in two.

"Kind of you to join us, son," his mother huffed. The other mother hens used her cluck as an excuse to continue their squawking. Their children, whose attendance, like his own, was compulsory, invented ways to pass their time under the nurture and admonition of a sharply parted comb-over and constant complaining for better behavior. Some played with loose fabric and frayed strings at coat ends and shirt seams before said distraction was smacked from their hands or lips. One of Cillian's classmates chewed her blond hair until it was brown. Some of the younger children watched the hypnotic rhythm of their feet bouncing against the edge of the couch cushion, or the occasional wisp of flame that found life with a passing draft over the coals.

Cillian recklessly enjoyed the ranch-covered jerky, ignoring all conversation until the noise of conversation overpowered his obnoxious chews and heated each face in the room faster than any coal fire could.

"Be careful with that talk, Mrs. Fairway. Subjects such as those get you kicked off the Parent/Teacher Finance Committee. I'm a living testament to that," Mrs. Trotsky warned. "Any departure from the status quo and they cry, 'Coup!'"

Mrs. Fairway, a young mother of three with smeared eye shadow and a rushed hair bun, cleared her throat and without looking saved her son from toppling over the blue suede couch closest to the fireplace. Cillian had forgotten the boy's name, but enjoyed watching a young man of adventure, like himself.

"We're not asking for much, here. Just the chance to fundraise on our own for an extra hands-on learning experience. A pottery class, archery lessons. I will even settle for a day here at the Clare farm, if they will have us, but we need to have a day for the third grade boys to be, well, *boys*. The period-based dress up parties have been fun and tasteful, but we all have a tough enough time keeping these boys in regular clothes, let alone waistcoats. And God forgive them for their conduct in togas," Mrs. Fairway lamented.

A confident and overrefined voice chimed in with a singsong reply. "Having raised a couple of well-cultured and well-behaved young men, I can sympathize with your concerns, Mrs. Fairway, but I believe you've overemphasized the importance of the *need*, as you put it, for such activities. We've seen many young men in our community go without, either by choice or necessity, those activities and they've turned out just as well-adjusted as my George and William."

"Thank you for your thoughtful and experienced opinion, Mrs. Schultz, but I think Mrs. Fairway may be more concerned with the lack of diversity in the children's activity days, as I am.

While these parties have been the subject of numerous topics and times, I am personally concerned with the lack of diversity in learning forms," Cillian's mother stated calmly.

Mrs. Schultz leaned forward over her crossed, hose-covered legs. Her rainbow-colored American flag amulet, usually hidden in a silicone crevasse, dangled forward and a few flakes of dried makeup floated to the floor when she spoke. "Surely, Cillian does not prefer a pigsty for his learning over a properly managed schoolroom?" Mrs. Schultz asked.

Mrs. Clare began to speak, but Cillian cut her short. "I've never learned in a pigsty, but I have been in all the classrooms. At least there's something new at the pigsty for me. Do you know of a good pigsty nearby, Mrs. Schultz?"

Mrs. Fairway stopped a clear laugh, but couldn't stop her snort. Mrs. Schultz sat back in the chair, mouth agape, leaving Cillian's comment suspended in the middle of the room, appalled by the adolescent affinity for filth. "I cannot say that I do know of any pigsties, Mr. Clare. And *good* pigsties, I'm sure they do not exist."

Cillian found it hard to believe that there were no good pigsties. He was sure where there were good pigs there would be good pigsties, much like the close correlation between good food and good cooks.

He thought the debate was far from over and prepared for rebuttal, but Mrs. Schultz readdressed the mothers. "I, for one, find it very unseemly to force the majority of the children to a field trip they would have no interest in, and frankly, that would yield no results other than general dirtiness. There is nothing essential to learn on any of these suggested excursions that would be beneficial to the children's progress, especially in a world as progressive as ours."

"That's hardly true, Mrs. Schultz," Cillian's mother objected. "Each of these trips can yield much good and could be very essential to those children who find a depth of interest that may lead to a career choice. I know they are only nine, but some nine-year-olds are aware of their lot."

"I grant you that. These boys and girls are an exceptional group, but if we want to raise the next *forward-thinking* generation, are we really doing our job by letting them play in the dirt, swim in creeks, and avoid the classroom at such formative ages? I'm very proud of the two young men I've raised and I know their paths were directly influenced by their academic experiences they had in the classroom and by all of the cultural events they enjoyed. In fact, they're both finding many opportunities in *respected* fields because of those experiences."

"We're very happy to hear George and Will are--"

"What do they do?" Cillian interrupted.

His mother snapped like a twig. "Cillian Patrick Clare, what have I said about interrupting?"

"A welcome interjection!" Mrs. Fairway said, smiling at Cillian Patrick Clare. "I'd also like to know the answer. It's been quite a long time since we have heard from the boys."

Mrs. Schultz hesitated, but warmly obliged after primly folding her hands and smiling, satisfied by another's interest in her momma-made boys. "George has landed a very fulfilling job as a costume designer for some of the most progressive plays in the Dallas and Austin area."

"What kind of plays? The ones with sword fightin'?" Cillian blurted and stabbed at an imaginary opponent.

"I've heard they're so progressive that they've dispensed with the costumes altogether," a nameless mother clucked.

There were short hysterics, but not enough to dent Mrs. Schultz's pride. Rather, it emboldened her with indignation and she doubled down on her heavy bet on progression. "Shakespeare was quite the rouse in his day and George says his playwright friends are nothing short of The Bard's brilliance in their own time. Will, on the other hand, has found wonderful work as a campaign manager for that economics professor who ran for a House seat. He's the one all the youngsters supported early in the election."

"Did he win?" Cillian asked. He ripped another ranch-soaked jerky piece off in his mouth and chewed voraciously.

"No, sadly, he did not."

"Why not?" Cillian asked.

Mrs. Schultz prepared a nuanced answer, but another anonymous answer relieved her. "His campaign ran out of money."

They all laughed at the expense of another Schultz boy. Mrs. Schultz slunk sullenly to the back of the armchair.

Trying to detect reddening in Mrs. Schultz's cheeks, Cillian found his efforts frustrated by a layer or three of make-up. Mrs. Schultz boiled quietly for the rest of the evening in a stew of her own making.

Cillian gnawed the rest of the jerky to a fine mush and swallowed it down in a disturbingly large lump. His mother chided him with a sideways glance and another finger snap. He bored of the debate over pigsties or progression.

Turning his attention to the window, Cillian caught a splendid glimpse of a gray fleecy cloud that spanned the sky, letting the sun peek past the gloomy curtain before speeding to the darkening edge of the eastern horizon, tinting the underside of the curtain with active rays. He felt the darkness and uselessness of the living room against the light, like peering through a cracked door into a celestial bedroom. Cillian's favorite part of each day would soon be past, filled with empty conversations and no action, an occurrence he found almost as repulsive and useless as eating vegetable soup. He cherished the golden evening light and planned to do what any pirate confronted with a difficult lock on a treasure chest would do. He used the dynamite.

"No more field trips! No more dress up parties!" He shouted, dropped his plate of jerky, and raised his fists in a victorious V above his head. The clucking house, silenced and surprised, looked on in panic as their chicks ran riot in all directions. Boys and girls, recounting the times they had been snapped at, told to hush, or pinched for their insubordination, reached their breaking point. Their mothers thought their gossiping gospels deserved more attention and respect than this, but the children saw fit to give them the same attention and respect that their mothers allowed them to show at Sunday morning services, which wasn't much at all.

No command, whistle, or grim look was heeded. Cillian, satisfied and encouraged, looked for more dynamite and found it quickly. "No more school!" he yelled. The other children stopped only to shout their affirmation and continued the mutiny. Shoes and shirts were removed and thrown. Cillian laughed joyously to see the Fairway boy dump himself over the back of the couch before his mother could stop him.

Cillian's mother gathered her wits and swiped twice at his neck, as if to wring him. She missed and cursed her side of the boy's genetic pedigree that made him so quick. He sprang out of the living room and set course for the mudroom. Every pirate knew his exits well. Cillian, being the little pirate that he was, knew he would waste no time with locks at the mudroom exit, but he had forgotten about the Admiral's ship that would likely be blockading the door—his father.

※

Cillian sneezed as a fresh gust of straw and scarlet barn dust filled his nostrils, nearly causing him to drop two full pails of water. He set them down while he gingerly checked his backside. A raised, red mark grew across his left buttock where his father's belt had landed. The right buttock remained virtually untouched. His father wasn't known for accuracy with a belt, but he could outrun most horses for a fair distance and cover himself with tractor grease faster than any other man Cillian had ever known.

"It ain't gonna get any better, if you keep staring at it. All my bumps and bruises go away quicker the more work I do. If you would have watered the pigs when I asked, you wouldn't have any stripes," his father said as he disappeared into the tool room in the corner of the barn. The clang of tools tossed across the concrete foundation meant Cillian had the chore of reorganizing the tool room after the correct tool was eventually found.

Cillian endured the squeak of his teeth grinding inside his mouth, composed himself, and rubbed his stripes of disobedience.

"Rubbin' don't help either. Have you decided how you'll ask your mother to forgive you?" His father's voice boomed from the tool room loud enough for Cillian to feel its force underfoot.

"No!" Cillian's voice cracked against the north wind. He cursed the air that took the *man* out of his voice.

"You better have it figured out before I come back in the house for dinner. She was in a wild huff when I left her and we'll be lucky to see salt and tomatoes on a plate. It appears Mrs. Frasier used your little outburst to swindle your mother out of that ham I smoked on Thursday."

Cillian fought the temptation to comment on the Frasier twins' eating habits, but anyone with reasonable discernment could deduce they wouldn't be winning any endurance competitions, unless they entered pie-eating contests.

He shimmied around the corner of the barn. Foot-sized drops of water splashed from his pails and over his shuffling feet. He was protected from the wind, but not the well water that iced his feet no matter the season.

He contemplated what he would say to his mother, without a doubt wanting to pacify her need for justice and still somehow avoid her wrath. He also hoped to add his own qualifiers to legitimize his actions, though not his piratical actions, of course. Action must be taken against the power-hungry mother's club before they moved in on his Boy Scout Troop, his baseball team, or any other group involving fun in the dirt. The iron-fisted hen party could never be allowed to influence his development from boyhood to manhood. While they could never rid the entire earth of those time-tested fundamentals so necessary to the life of a coming-of-age boy, they could surely bar him and all his friends from them until it was too late. He shivered against freezing feet and the fear of losing his manhood before it began.

He wished for Meadow's encouraging presence and fine counsel in these trying moments. Her father must have been late delivering his weekly feed route. The Clares were the last stop on his route and he didn't have time to drop her off in the morning during the frigid, dead months when feed and service were most precious.

Cillian strained to bear the weight of his mother's disappointment alone and considered escaping, yet again, beyond the creek and into imagination, but she must be made wary of the mortal danger the mothers posed to his development. His father would naturally agree with him, being a man, but only if Cillian's apology was strong enough to withstand his mother's objection to his behavior. He must lay bare his conduct, admit his disobedience and shortcomings, and defend his *need* for manly field trips. He not only desired fresh air and the chance to sweat, he *needed* it.

He finished filling the trough with water and left a shovel nearby, knowing he would be required to break the ice in the morning before church. He readied himself with a short prayer for wisdom, knowing it could be granted to even the smallest and weakest if only they humbled themselves into asking. He marched to the house with sloshing steps and a ready mind.

His mother practiced the art of suspense when exacting her discipline against disobedience. To have her children sweat out their worry over when her outburst would occur was never enough. She tallied their misdeeds better than Santa and made coal a desirable reward for misbehavior. Tonight Mrs. Clare slow-cooked her rage with careful thought and a blow-by-blow recall of her son's sins that Cillian found remarkable. He hoped he could inherit half of her memorization skills.

She hurriedly finished breakfast-for-dinner, her go-to when short of time and ingredients. Bacon made its presence known to all in the house in possession of working noses and ears. Cillian resisted the temptation to steal a few fresh strips. It would only make the coming storm more severe.

He avoided her gaze by using the opposite side of the hearth he had before his mutiny, his back turned towards her, to warm his feet. Still wearing his socks, he enjoyed the ghostly disappearance of the wet footprints as the heat of the hearth evaporated the dirty water and left a dusty imprint in its place. His feet warmed and his stomach growled. Soon, his mother would call for the family to "get it while it's hot." He softly whistled the tune of his mother's favorite hymn in hopes she would hear, repeat the lyrics to herself, and calm her mind, as she did when frustrated with those whom she could not discipline. He whistled through three verses like a good Baptist boy, but heard no accompaniment from the kitchen.

She did hear, but disregarded. She wanted her rage unchecked by the calm and meek mind of the hymn writer. There was no peace to be had in her house tonight until her grievances were heard and her wrath spent.

"It's ready," came the shout from the kitchen. Cillian prayed shortly, again.

Cal filled his plate with an omelet, bacon, and biscuits with sand plum jelly spread from the previous year's picking. He walked without the weight of the day's work on his shoulders and settled comfortably in a wood chair his own grandfather had made. He was aware of the coming conflict and was determined to enjoy a few bites and moments of peace before the battle began. Few things tasted better than a breakfast raised and slaughtered at one's own hand.

Too scared to leave his perch, Cillian continued to switch his feet upon the hearth with an ever-quickening rhythm. Even though sweat ran from his ankles to his soles, he refused to face the heat of the kitchen.

His father watched his nervous steps for a few moments and called, "Come get your dinner, Cillian."

Cillian knew the verdict, even before the court was commanded to rise for the reading of "guilty on all counts."

He hopped off the hearth with forced enthusiasm. He moved toward the kitchen with what felt like normal pace, but nothing felt as it should. His feet were numb to the bend and creak of the wood floor. He no longer smelled bacon or baked biscuits. He tried to think of eggs, but could only think of shame.

Shame, he knew, in these moments was right and required, but he hated it anyway. He hated the singling out of his mistakes over those of others, as if his faults carried more weight than the crimes read by an evening news anchor. He hated the helpless and hopeless feeling of being wrong without the chance of being able to repair things at his own hand. He hated the destruction he caused and never understood his mother's need to augment the shame he felt for acting like *a boy*.

There should be more shame for boys who don't act like boys, he thought.

He turned the corner to the kitchen and grabbed a paper plate without acknowledging his mother's glare or the glorious smell of bacon and eggs. He ignored the awesome oppression of her indignant look and tried not to audibly appreciate the beauty of bacon now that he stood before it. He went to the omelet first, thinking his mother would soften her blows for the boy who went selflessly last for the bacon.

Before he could stab the thinnest omelet, a greased spatula parried his fork away. "Do you think you deserve a meal?" his mother growled.

"No." His voice cracked, but his countenance portrayed a confidence and surety he did not own.

"Why don't you deserve a meal, Cillian Clare?" she asked calmly, staying her wrath for the correct moment.

"Because I caused a ruckus, earlier," he admitted. The shame now dictated his demeanor. His shoulders drooped and his gaze pointed to the floor through the blurry lens of tears.

"Not only did you cause a ruckus. You have assured yourself no other activity, except for Mrs. Schultz's dress-up. She used your little ruse to convince everyone, with the exception of Mrs. Fairway and myself, that you need more structure and etiquette in your activities. And, as if that weren't enough, she has used her newfound influence to set up one meeting per month that I am to attend at her gaudy house. She has ensured a way to waste at least one Saturday of each month. If I have to attend these meetings, then so do you, mister. What do you have to say for yourself?"

"I'm sorry for what I did. Will you forgive me, Momma?"

Her voice rose in volume and pitch. "Your complete disrespect for adults discussing serious matters has landed me in responsibilities that I do not have the time for and you will suffer them with me. Do you hear me?"

Cillian submissively bowed his head. "Please, forgive me, Momma."

"You'll go with me to these meetings and you'll starve with the rest of us because I don't have time to cook dinner on those Saturdays. And, don't you dare assume you'll get out of your weekend chores just because you won't be here for most of the day!"

His father tried to stop the diatribe. "Momma," he said.

"Please, Momma," Cillian begged. Tears flowed freely and he raked them from his face with angry swipes.

"Now we'll both have to go to Mrs. Schultz's *estate,* and I'll be forced to sit under judgey looks from those god-awful family portraits! I'll be forced by the Rules of Niceties to bring a well-baked pie or sweet that won't be touched because one witch whispered to all the other witches and I'll take it home to my shame!"

"Momma!" Cal Clare commanded her attention.

Cillian clenched his fists and tried to grind his crowns to fine powder.

His mother heard the squeak of his tiny teeth. "You wouldn't grind them teeth if you had any sense to know what unneeded stress you've brought to this house."

"Sarah Clare!" His father resorted to shouting. Cal's face showed no rage, no disappointment, only a need to command and control the atmosphere.

Cillian and Sarah turned warily to Cal and his authority, fearful of his disappointment and judgment.

"Cillian, you'll be punished for your disobedience. Your mother will settle on the right amount of punishment and I'll make sure it's carried out."

Cal paused, swigged a gulp of tea, and continued. "Sarah, do not blame the boy for something outside of his control. He gave Mrs. Schultz her chance, sure, but she would have found another opportunity with or without his help." Sarah crossed her arms and rolled her eyes, but Cal continued. "I told you it was a bad idea to get involved with *that* group of women, long ago. Now seems as good a time as any to leave them to the yield of their own harvest. We'll take our children on their own activities. We need to send a clear message to our children about how they are to learn. That responsibility falls wholly upon us, even if we have them for only a few vital hours during each day. Are we agreed?"

Sarah's demeanor was rigid and obstinate, but she couldn't, at present, deny or adequately argue any point contrary to Cal's. "We are," she said. Exhausted from the afternoon of needless battles disguised as care between passive-aggressive mothers, she caved to his judgment, knowing it held much more valuable insight than misdirected vitriol. Words and passion meant for her peers had fallen to the capable, but small emotional shoulders of Cillian.

Cillian stood at his mother's side, arms straight, tears dammed by eyelids and lashes, determined to remain unbroken by an opponent, even if that opponent was his mother.

"Thank you, love." Pleased, Cal gulped down brackish tea and chewed through overdone bacon with an enjoyment that Cillian found barbaric. "As for you, little Cill, we'll handle our business when I'm done with Momma's best breakfast yet."

Cillian sweated through his breakfast. Either his mother had added vengeful jalapeños to his omelet or he anticipated the sting of leather upon flesh.

Cillian bit through a shout before it began. His legs clenched against an agony he was not prepared to express. He would not show his defeat, not even in his punishment.

"What's the game this time? Shed No Tear?" Cal asked.

Cillian glared at his father, who held the thickest leather belt Cillian had ever seen then or since.

Cal raised an eyebrow. "If I'm not mistaken, I'd say that face was meant for me. Though I know it's more for yourself than anyone else. What did you lose today, Cill?"

"Nothing. I got caught," Cillian said curtly, rubbing his backside with vigor. He had indeed bested Mrs. Schultz and caused a child riot that defeated every mother at the meeting, but he could never defeat his parents' ultimate advantage—authority. He didn't have it and he wanted it for the sole purpose of being better than anyone who opposed him.

"There's nothing wrong with wanting to win," Cal said.

"Apparently there is." Cillian defied his father with full voice and puffed chest, perched above wobbling knees.

Amused by his son's determination, Cal chuckled. "Of course there isn't, but there is a flaw to how you tried to win when you chose to use malice in your game. You wanted to win for the wrong reason."

Cillian scraped tears from his face before they left their shameful streaks. He resolved that defiant silence was his best move. He refused to confirm or deny his father's observations, regardless of their accuracy. The pirate within him threatened to overtake his soul and sail away toward a life of rebellion.

His father held his breath and stared down the little pirate. "Go get your jacket and boots," he said.

A finicky flood light made the swine's thick hairs luminescent. They protruded like crystalline stalks from their milky hide. The piglets mixed together in the mud under their mother in a myriad of spotted fur. Cillian found the differences between the siblings peculiar and hopeful because he didn't want to look or act like his peers. The big Duroc, who Cillian had named Ferdinand due to his childhood confusion about the difference between a pig and a bull, kept to himself in the corner of the neighboring pen, apart from his mate and her litter. He stood alert, agitated by a coyote frenzy in the distance.

Cillian balanced on the second pipe fence rail, which was in dire need of sandblasting and paint. His father dumped a bag of pellets into a trough for the nursing mother. She splashed through the muck and stomped over her litter to enjoy the trough treasure in violent joy. Cillian winced when she ran over her litter, but she managed to avoid them every time with an innate knowledge of each piglet's presence.

"What do you think?" Cal asked.

Cillian blocked the stench from his nose and mouth with a sleeve-covered hand. "I wouldn't eat it," he said with a muffled voice.

Cal chuckled. "Not the pellets. What do you think of their pigsty?"

"It stinks! And, she could lose one of the piglets under the mud or a puddle."

"No. They squeal too loud to ever be lost, even under water and mud. Do you think it's a good pigsty?"

Cillian analyzed the size and contents of the small pen. It was small for his tastes, but the piglets and sow didn't seem bothered. The interior was equal parts dry, wet, muddy, and sloppy, with cloven hoof prints scattered and innumerable. "What makes it a good pigsty, Daddy?"

Cal scratched his beard, enjoying the critique. "Well, first things first. Are the pigs doing what pigs do best?"

"What do they do best?" Cillian asked.

"Are they wallowing, snorting, squealing, and eating regularly?"

Cillian searched the pen again and witnessed all activities as they had been rightly described. "Yep."

"Are they healthy? Do you hear any wheezes, see any limps, or smell anything awful?"

Cillian observed again. "No wheezes or limps, but I always smell something awful here."

"That's the awful smell of life. We're looking for the awful smell of death. They're different, and you don't so much smell death as much as you feel it."

Knowing what life smelled like, Cillian confirmed the likes of life around the pen, but dreaded the day he would encounter death. "I don't think I smell death," he said, timidly.

"You're right. There's no death. I'll keep you from that smell as long as I can, but someday you must know it," Cal said with temperature equal to that of the air.

Cillian shivered and placed the cold metal of his jacket zipper to his lips. He stared blankly at the playing piglets, meditating on the truth that they must all enjoy what they do best before they died, as he must, and that he was partially responsible for their enjoyment.

"What do you think, Cill? Good pigsty or not?"

Cillian nodded. His thoughts were lost on the proper function of all the farm's residents before they passed, even the farmer.

"I agree, Cill. It's a pretty good pigsty."

Just Wages

"You get a dime for the pigweeds and a quarter for every thistle you dig up and bring back to me," Cal Clare said.

Cillian shouldered a shovel and assured a firm grip over the splintering handle. The morning's humidity and heat warmed his mustard-colored deerskin gloves, causing his scrawny fingers to sweat and slip within.

"Why's it so hot already?" Cillian whined.

"The sun is a morning person in the spring and summer," Cal said. "You can pick the weeds until lunch."

Cillian turned and marched toward his morning task.

"Don't you want the wheelbarrow so you can carry more back at a time?" Cal asked.

Without qualification or reason, Cillian said with undue confidence, "Nope."

Cal shook his head and disappeared back into the barn. His antique Ford tractor had sputtered to a standstill for the third morning in a row and he returned to his tire-kicking. Cillian set out across the gravel drive in front of their house. Clover and henbit dotted their lawn in lush patches above the bashful Bermuda. His mother grew peppers and herbs in flower beds at the base of their pine porch. Cottonwood seeds floated like fiber clouds in the dead air above the lawn. Some of them tumbled to the shaggier sections of the weeds and nestled comfortably in the early greenery until rains would drive them to the dirt in the late spring. The weeds would have their glory in the remains of spring, but

Bermuda would hold victory in the scorch of summer that was fast approaching. Cillian kicked the purple tops of the henbit, sending their sour and saccharine stench into the humid air.

His plan was simple enough for the day. He thought it best to swath over their block of property in a series of circular patterns each week until the herbal menace was eradicated and today, being the first weeding mission of the year, he would start with the smallest swath. If he finished as early as he hoped, there would be time for a swim in the creek before lunch. He did not care too much for the money he would earn as long as he saved enough for a new baseball mitt before midsummer. His old Rawlings was flaky and he feared the stitching wouldn't last past his team's long stretch of tournaments in June.

Pleasant thoughts of new glove scent and chewing on fresh stitching were interrupted by the familiar clamor of a diesel delivery truck that carried the week's feed, more useless tools his father had ordered, and a particular red-headed friend of his. The truck's chipped ivory hood was fastened to the bumper by a bungee cord and the storage container rocked from side to side each time the tires plunged into a new pothole, threatening to throw the truck on its side. Cillian imagined how much his daddy would cuss if the truck did tip over and destroy the new fence.

His mother's peach trees lined the drive and darkened the cab each time it passed one. The sheen of the girl's hair in the passenger seat alternated ribbons of fire and shade each time the sun graced the cab and again died away behind each shadow. The truck, having passed all potholes, roared and rushed into the circular drive, skidding to a stop. Miniature mounds of gravel piled in front of each tire. Cillian rolled his eyes, knowing the chore of leveling out the mounds would fall to him in the afternoon.

Meadow leaped from the passenger side and slammed the door behind her. Cillian could only see her sullied socks, gaunt, pale calves, and tattered tennis shoes in the gap between the truck's undercarriage and the ground. Her feet stabbed tiny depressions into the loose gravel. She rounded the front of the truck with the sun shining through her auburn curls. Cillian always likened her hair to dry kindling suddenly catching fire when the sun's light found it. It surprised the beholder and seemed to warm the air around her. She sprinted up to him, stopped short to kick the mauve tops of henbit as he had moments before.

"What's up, Silly Cilly? Where are you going with that shovel?" Meadow asked.

"I'm clearing out the pigweeds and thistles on the property."

Meadow frowned and folded her arms. "Darn. I hoped Smith and Wesson had killed another armadillo and you were going to bury it. Do you remember when they killed that skunk and brought it to your back porch?"

Cillian laughed and dropped the blade into the soft spring soil. He rested his hands atop the splintered shaft. "Yup. Daddy barely kept Momma from shooting both of them with a .22."

Meadow turned and waved at her father, who was on his way to talk to Cal. She turned back to Cillian and spoke with her normal excitable tone. "I'm here for the day so can I help you with the thistles and pigweeds."

Prepared to say no and pocket the cash promised to him, Cillian thought for a moment how Meadow might be able to help him make more money. In order to be fair he would have to pay her what she would agree to. "Will you take a nickel for each pigweed and a dime for each thistle you get?"

Meadow curled her lower lip and scraped her heel in the clover until it smelled and looked as appetizing as cooked spinach. "Do I get to keep the flowers from each thistle I pick?" she asked, warily, as if she were worried that her request may be too much.

"I'll even give you the flowers from the thistles I pick," Cillian agreed, readily.

They both spat and shook on it. Meadow turned and started running toward the barn.

"We're going to the fields!" Cillian shouted after her.

"We're gonna need wheelbarrows, Cill," she yelled without turning to see his grimace and tightening grip upon the handle.

ℬ

Dew passed from long Bermuda blades to their lower legs, soaking Cillian's socks and Meadow's now bare feet as they moved from their first hill to the next. One trip to unload their wheelbarrows had already been made and with only a fourth of the barrow's space left for each of them, another dumping trip looked likely. The sun, with intensity fit for summer, had risen high enough to shed light on the opposite sides of all the roofs on the prairie, signaling midmorning. Locusts, which were silent or played their laggardly tunes in the early mornings, came alive under the shade of the grass. Occasionally the children's steps would find a mole trail and Cillian would mention how he wished there was a hose long enough to reach out from the barn to the mole's trail so he could drown out the subterranean critters. Pigweeds and thistles were plentiful. Cillian salivated, thinking he may be able to buy a mitt and a football on their next trip to the city. He thanked God for making both of the nuisance weeds easily identifiable. Pigweeds with their bloody stalks and thistles with their fuzzed purple buds added unique color and texture to the prairie, but to Cillian and Meadow they acted as beacons for more coin.

They cut down what they could of a large thistle patch near a lone hackberry and rested under its shade when they grew weary. Cillian climbed to a low branch full of ripe berries that had been overlooked by the birds and squirrels through the winter. He harvested the thin branches with his pocket knife and dropped them to Meadow below. Meadow rushed a few of the berries into her mouth and began to chew.

"Ow!" She spat out the exclamation along with the berries. "They're hard!"

Climbing down from his perch, Cillian laughed and said, "Don't chew the middle. You're supposed to nibble off the soft, sweet shell. The hard part is the seed. Momma said you can crush them up into a paste or make milk out of them, but you don't chew them."

Cillian laid down next to their bounty. He enjoyed removing the shell and soft part and spitting the hard seed as far as he could. Meadow sat and gnawed away the shells with care. "Are we supposed to keep the seeds for paste and milk?" she asked.

"Nah, Momma doesn't make it. She said it's what the Indians used to do for medicine."

Meadow stood with a full branch in her hand and looked back to Cillian's home. Their property and the land around it was quiet and seemed content to soak up the sun after drinking the night's dew. "You think a war party ever came up to this very tree to rest after fighting off cavalrymen?" Meadow asked.

Cillian rolled to his stomach in time to see a squirrel scurry up the hackberry to the spot where he had just harvested from. "I don't know. It's possible. They probably needed more than berries after a good fight, though."

"I'd want a couple plates of spaghetti after a good fight!" Meadow punched the air like a boxer preparing for a bout.

Cillian observed how his warm breath moved the light pieces of the dark loam near the base of the tree. "You always want spaghetti," he said drily.

Bored with shadow boxing an imaginary opponent and distracted by hunger, Meadow rubbed her scrawny torso. "Speaking of spaghetti, what's your momma making for lunch? I'm starving."

Cillian popped a handful of berries into his mouth and stored them in his cheek like sunflower seeds. "I don't know. She doesn't tell me. I just show up and eat."

"Do you think she'd be mad if we showed up early?" Meadow asked, hopeful.

૪ઌ

Cillian convinced Meadow to cut down, haul, and dump two more trips worth of weeds with him before showing up for an early lunch. Sarah Clare welcomed them with an assortment of deli meats, cheeses, and homemade bread. Cillian ate his fill, but Meadow, who continued her hungry complaining, was sent away with one of Cillian's cartoon-themed lunch pails laden with bread, peanut butter, Chickasaw plum jelly, and a knife for spreading. Annoyed that his mother let Meadow borrow his favorite pail, Cillian quietly felled many thistles and pigweed, a little Paul Bunyan of the prairie. He worked until near midday without taking much notice of his companion. He was no longer annoyed, but his body was given to the labor and his mind entertained his regular daydreams of baseball games and pirate adventures. Meadow's frustrated whines and huffs woke him from a particularly enjoyable daydream about a glory-filled life on the high seas. He cleared the sweat from his face and pulled his wet hair back from blocking his view, watching Meadow struggle with the idiot stick against a pigweed stalk that was as thick as a fence post. He hurdled toward Meadow over the thick hide of Bermuda grass that covered the hills and had been ignored by the hay cutters in the autumn. She struggled almost to the point of crying and slammed the idiot stick against the stalk recklessly.

"Step back," Cillian commanded.

Meadow retreated in surprised fear rather than response to his command and watched as Cillian placed the blade of his shovel into the gnarled groove she had created with the idiot stick, heeled the step, and drove his full weight and momentum through the base of the stalk. He kept the almost tree sized weed from falling to the ground and spreading its seed by grabbing a smooth section on the stalk that was surrounded by barbs. The base of the severed stalk shimmered and reflected the intense sunlight like a piece of glass pointed at Cillian's face. He squinted against the reflection, found another clear section of stalk to grip, and lifted the behemoth weed over the edge of the nearby barrow.

"You take this," he said, offering Meadow the shovel for the remainder of their work.

"Are we almost done?" Meadow asked.

Cillian never knew Meadow to shy away from work or activities and found her question to be against her nature. "See that fence over there?" Cillian pointed to a wood posted barbed-wire fence seventy-five yards to the east. "When we reach that, we will be done."

"Good," Meadow muttered. She was clearly relieved and thankful their work was nearing its end.

Her words and demeanor made Cillian more than curious. Any other day he'd have to drag her home across the pastures, Meadow being barefooted and obstinate as usual. "Why is that good?" he asked.

Meadow shrugged and the corners of her mouth turned down to her jaw line. "No reason," she said.

"You have something better to do?" he asked.

Meadow crossed her arms at his question that doubled as an accusation. "Nope," she said curtly and tilted her head to the north, showing Cillian her annoyance with him would only be inflamed by the mere sight of him.

"That's good to hear 'cause I think I wanna work till dark, now. It's not that hot today and we're pretty close to a water hose so there's no reason to quit, yet."

The news washed over Meadow like ice water. She neither moved nor responded for a few long moments, allowing the locusts to speak for her. She knew she was trapped, but she tried to force a gap in the conversation. "I may have to leave early and let you finish the work. Daddy—"

Cillian interrupted her with a finger wag. "You told me earlier you were here for the day."

"Maybe I'm getting a little tired." The tone of her declaration made it sound more like a question.

"You've always said, 'Meadow never gets tired!' And, you've said it twice today when I asked if you needed a break. What is the *real* reason you want to cut out early?" he demanded.

Meadow fancied herself the swamp rabbit and Cillian the owl. The routes of escape were endless, but few were probable. She searched frantically for an angle she could beat him at or a hole he couldn't fit in.

"Don't run, Meadow. Just tell me why you wanna go in so early," he pleaded.

Meadow felt inclined to answer with some of the truth, owing Cillian's loyal friendship at least part of the truth. "There's a show I wanna watch."

Cillian had tried for some time to convince her to watch some Saturday cartoons with him. He viewed this admission as a first step toward finally convincing her of the entertainment value of cartoons and he struggled to contain his joy. His feet grew giddy and his hands moved rapidly about him as he spoke. "Finally! What show is it? *Scooby-Doo*? *Ninja-Turtles*? No, please, let it be *Batman*?" He paused for a moment of worry when she had not confirmed his best guesses. "Don't tell me it's *Rugrats* or something like that."

"No, it's not any of those." Her voice was feeble and seasoned with shame.

"Well, which cartoon is it?"

"It's not a cartoon."

"Reruns of the *Little Rascals*?"

Meadow shook her head and played with the prairie between her toes.

"*The Three Stooges*?" he almost begged, knowing he would react poorly if the show were what he feared.

Meadow did not look up. Lock after lock of hair shrouded her face in a fiery curtain. "Nope," she muttered.

Cillian hated unneeded suspense of this sort and despised her unwillingness to divulge what seemed like trivial information. "Just tell me!" he shouted.

Meadow shouted back in defiance of his heavy-handedness. "It's *7th Heaven!*"

Cillian's accusative tone and hands abated. His body, taut with anxiety, slackened in despair. He retrieved the idiot stick he had tossed to his side at some point during their exchange, pulled his feet through the dead grass, and set about his work like a drone. Embarrassed by his friend's choice of entertainment and unsure how to address the problem he had with dramatic teenage shows, he worked toward the east fence in silence. Meadow followed, embarrassed by her forced admission that she was entertained by anything remotely girly.

※

Cillian dumped the last of his haul in a weed pile next to the barn. His father emerged from the dim shadow of the barn's interior. A low-hanging cloud of dust and two muddied Australian Shepherds followed him, nipping the air around each other's noses. Cillian laughed at them.

"They've been tussling all day. What's the damage?" Cal asked.

"Two hundred and seventy-five pigweeds and one hundred and three thistles."

Cal calculated the total in his head and his eyes widened with surprise when he became aware of the total. "Fifty-three dollars and a quarter. I'll have to go dig some out of the cash stash." He left the pair standing awkwardly next to the pile under the lone magnolia tree on the property.

Cillian waited patiently for his father to return, leaning against the side of his barrow and kicking away Smith and Wesson when their conflict wandered too close to his ankles. Meadow wrote imaginary figures on the palm of her left hand with her right index finger. The sun sat at its apex for the day. The shade under the magnolia tree's thick leaves was much cooler than the direct sunlight. A light breeze brought the stomach-curdling stench from the pigs that resided on the east side of the barn. Cillian, reminded of a tune by the return of the spring songbirds, hummed and drummed a beat on the side of the barrow with his palms. He delighted through two verses before Meadow interrupted with an obnoxious clearing of her throat. Cillian stopped and found Meadow's skin had turned a fearsome shade of flushed pink and her cheeks were blotched blood-red.

"I ain't no fool, Cillian Clare," Meadow growled. Smith and Wesson halted their snipping, faced Meadow, and tucked their tails.

Cillian laughed. "You could have fooled me. Wait, what are you talking about?"

She pointed the index finger she had used for her calculations at him like a readied weapon. "You're only paying me half of what you're getting paid for each weed!"

"Close. I'm actually getting paid more than double for the thistles, but remember you get to keep the flowers from everything thing we picked today," Cillian said. His assertiveness swelled and shrouded his earlier issue he took with her preference for *7th Heaven*.

"That ain't fair at all! Are you paying me half of what you make because *I'm a girl*?"

Cillian could not let the accusation of his vainglorious deceit on account of her gender go unaddressed. "Not at all. I'm paying you twice as much as I would anyone else. You work harder on your lazy days than most of my friends."

"Then why am I only getting half of what you're making?" she asked with the hint that no answer he could present would whet her appetite.

"Because those are the prices we agreed to." Cillian ironed his words so flat that their edge cut into Meadow's feelings.

Cal tramped across the lawn and driveway with their wages. His greasy jeans were half tucked in to steel-toed boots. A sullied shirt from his high school years rested on his shoulder and acted as a towel for his hands when he needed it. He came upon them with his normal expression that was not a clear smile, but nonetheless displayed his pleasure and contentedness with life. He sifted through crinkled bills and recounted them with deep whispers. He lowered the money to his son. "Fifty-three and a quarter. I'd say that makes us square."

Cillian nodded and counted the bills, not for accuracy but in adoration.

Cal sensed Meadow's silence and found her in a rigid rage. "What's got you boiling?" he asked.

"I ain't square," she said. Her gaze was fixed on the cash in Cillian's hand.

"You keep gritting those teeth that hard they're gonna turn to dust. Why aren't you square?" Cal asked, calmly. He discerned the problem at hand without having to hear her answer.

"Cillian is only paying me half of what you paid him per weed!"

Cillian interjected, "I'm actually getting paid more than double for the thistles."

Cal lifted a hand to quiet Cillian and focused on Meadow, whose distress worsened with each word Cillian spoke. "Did he tell you he would pay you more than what you're getting now?" Cal asked.

Meadow tossed her curls away from her face with a flick of her head. "No."

"Did you agree to the prices?"

"Yes, but he never said anything about how much he was getting paid for each weed."

Cal turned back to his son. "Why didn't you tell her your pay?"

Cillian shrugged. "She never asked. I don't have to tell her, but I would have told her if she would have asked."

Cal scratched his neck. His fingernails left grimy streaks near the collar of his gray shirt. He wore no robe, but he presided over this case as judge, nonetheless. "The only way to resolve this is that he pay what he agreed to pay."

"But, how is that fair, Uncle Cal?" Meadow pleaded. "I did the same work and I'm getting paid half."

"It's fair because you agreed to it. The only harm that comes from this will be the harm you work up because of your discontent. Take your money and agree to something better next time," Cal said. Convinced his judgment was sound, he resumed his pleased expression.

Cillian offered Meadow her just wages for one hundred and thirty pigweeds and fifty thistles felled. Meadow snatched the money from his hand begrudgingly and muttered under her breath, "Never gonna work with you again." She stomped off across the driveway and lawn, no doubt looking to appeal the judgment with Cillian's mother.

Cillian rested his hip on the wheelbarrow, counted his earnings once more, and smiled. Cal watched his son intently. Knowing envy guided Meadow's steps, he sought out his son's motives. "That's a lot of money for a fella your age. What are you gonna do with it?"

Cillian stuffed the money deep into the pocket of his jeans. "My Rawlings is old. I need to get a new one before the summer is over."

"There will be plenty more days to weed the fields. You won't make everything you need, today. Why don't you split the money with Meadow?" Cal asked.

"You even said that I was right to pay her what I did," Cillian protested.

"Yes, and you're still right. I would even go as far to say she's wrong to envy after more than she was paid, but generosity can salvage a friendship."

Cillian grew serious and considered the counsel. "You don't think she will want to be my friend anymore."

Cal hocked a loogie and spat it into the weed pile. "She may not go that far, but envy is a heavy and sharp-edged wedge that can cleave through the bones of some of the greatest friendships."

"What do you think I should do?" Cillian asked.

"That's not for me to lay on you, son. Your decision is yours to own." Happy with his statement and trusting his son to come to a worthy conclusion, Cal returned to the barn and his disagreeable tractor.

Cillian shoved his fists down into his pockets and played with the cash while wondering how to handle his broken fellowship. Meadow had charged across the lawn by now and had been presenting her testimony to a new judge in the kitchen. Cillian feared there may be a dispute between these judges that could spoil the atmosphere and food during dinner. His initial inclination was to offer Meadow his best insults, bore from careful thought, rather than extra compensation, but knew, from his playground experiences, that insults rarely worked well as a salve for wounded sensibilities. He started for the house without a plan. He only knew he must act to help mend what had been severed.

The sun tilted westward and warmed the southwest wind that blew directly into Cillian's face, a light breeze that soothed rather than abraded his skin. Tall prairie grasses played their whispered melody through the peaks and valleys of the surrounding hills. Cillian kicked the henbit once more, driving the scents up into the breeze and away through the hill's song.

Meadow stormed out of the house to meet him, slamming the screen door behind her and bypassing the steps to the porch by leaping directly onto the lawn. She covered the open ground between them in just a few charging strides. She stopped directly in front of him and leaned her grimace near the end of his nose. She breathed heavily through her freckled nostrils and showered Cillian with overheated breath.

"You wait till my daddy hears what you did!" she shouted.

Cillian retreated a step, reached into his pocket, and said, "I've decided to split the money with you since you split the work with me. You also get to keep the thistle buds. I just want us to be friends." He offered her the rest of the other half of the earnings.

Most of Meadow's malice receded and what was left was reserved for the embarrassment she felt. She lifted the peace offering gingerly from his hand. She did not bother to count it. She trusted his math. "I don't like being tricked, Cillian."

"I didn't trick you," he said with a light laugh and friendliness that eased Meadow's tone.

"It made me feel stupid. I don't like feeling stupid," she mumbled.

"Me either."

Awkward silence persisted between them for a short time until Cillian asked, "You hungry for more hackberries?"

§

Virginia Creeper

Parkinson's had folded Donald in many different ways in the last decade and Gwen was there to watch. Ten years with her late husband, Terry, had flown past her, but he could walk, talk, and comfort her. Donald shook for the first five years and sat rigid and speechless for the latter five.

The morning they removed his feeding tube, the nurse allowed Gwen to help bathe him for the last time. His two sons were scheduled to visit him as he starved in his chair, but Gwen continually prayed that something would take him before either of them arrived. She set out colorful canvases she had painted for him in their first few years, when the shaking began, and the speech was stuttered. Each time she brought a new painting into his room, she searched his face for a reaction, but each time she found a slack jaw and unperceiving eyes. Between showings of watercolors and pastels, she sat close to Donald in an old, cedar armchair covered with saddle blankets and watched the wind rustle the Virginia creeper vines on the solitary oak on the front lawn. She shivered each time the vine was yanked left or right by the breeze. She imagined how many times she would have had a terrible reaction from accidentally handling the vine, if this was her lawn. She would have no one to care for her as she tore at her own skin and soothed the rash under scalding waters with no one to stop her. Here, at Primrose Escapes, there was always someone on call to stop you from hurting yourself.

Donald's oldest son, born William and dubbed Dubby, strutted through the door in the afternoon a day after they pulled Donald's feeding tube. Gwen heard the click of his new dress shoes coming from down the tile hallway, but thought it was Vickie, who lived in the room next door, with a new pair of heels. Dubby was barrel-chested, much like Donald when Gwen had met him, but instead of a solid foundation to sit upon, Dubby's stomach spilled over his needlessly tight navy slacks like the cake icing he loved so much. He dragged a metal chair closer, its feet screeching on the floor, and forced a squinted smile. He sat.

"How are we this afternoon?" he asked.

Dying, Gwen thought, but restrained her tongue.

"What has it been, a week or two?" he asked.

"You came in October. It's now June," she said. Her tone was flat and curt.

"Well, you know how a dealership can be. They won't even let you off for church these days. In fact, Sabbaths usually bring the biggest commission. How have you been since then, *Gwen?*" He always said her name as if she was caught some place she shouldn't be.

"I've lived well and in fine company." She laid a few delicate fingers on Donald's decrepit knee. Donald's figure remained rigid and folded. His vital signs monitor continued its steady chirping.

Dubby leaned back on the chair's plastic back. It whined and cracked. He forced another smile. This time the fat above his cheekbones completely covered his eyes. "I'm glad he has matured into *fine company.*"

Gwen turned her welling eyes toward the Virginia creeper in order to feel less irritated and icky. She watched it sway in the wind that came from the valleys of the Wichita Mountains. Of all the places she imagined she would end up, her youthful self would likely have scolded her for ending up here with a dying man twenty years her senior. She had no friends. The nurses whispered that she was some sort of land grabber. Donald's longhorns and land had long ago been auctioned off to keep him alive until his brother William, whom Dubby was named after, felt guilty about the family fortune being drained through a feeding tube. His power of attorney made this Donald's last week. He never bothered to phone ahead and warn Gwen.

Gwen wanted community and friends, but the town was short on friendliness and the community centered in a couple of churches that struggled with a live-in friend of the opposite sex, regardless of the reasons she gave them for being there and caring for him.

"Fine company," Dubby muttered again and looked at his smart watch. "These things are modern marvels. I can categorize my incoming calls between serious buyers and cheap hagglers." He chuckled.

Not thinking the humor and laughter to be appropriate for a son in this situation, Gwen ignored Dubby and let her head hang above her bosom. The emerald-studded trinity necklace that Donald had bought her ten years prior dangled over her chest. Dubby came back to his polite senses.

"What will you do when this is over, Gwen?" he asked. He struggled for solemnity in the presence of his father, but Gwen appreciated him trying.

She gave a nervous giggle and shrug. "I honestly don't know."

Dubby leaned over his stomach, puzzled. "What about friends and family back home?"

Gwen frowned and shook her head. "I'm my parents' only child. Momma had seven miscarriages before me. I have no kids. I'm more barren than she was. Friends were scarce and the few that were close are now far off or passed."

She could tell how bleak it all sounded by the look on Dubby's face. She had to admit that, when she considered her situation, there wasn't much to be optimistic about. She held out hope for mysterious ways.

"Well, I could do something for you." The words seemed to spill out of him without his own control and Gwen sensed he wished he could grab them and put them back before she had heard them.

"What is that?" she asked, curious as to what he was really willing to sacrifice out of his life. She doubted she could get him to give her his shimmering Sterling Corvette.

"Well, what do you think you would need? I'm sure I could pay for a plane ticket to get to one of them far off friends. Maybe I could talk the nursing home manager into letting you rent this room?" He paused to read Gwen's expression. She stared at him with eerie patience. "I'm sure we'll think of something."

Gwen nodded and smiled, satisfied to know Dubby wasn't too cold to offer help, but that she was correct in guessing he would likely be too dumb to execute any. They spent the rest of the afternoon discussing everything with the exception of Donald. Gwen was disgusted with the conversation and with herself for engaging in it, but she knew that Dubby couldn't handle any talk about his father. He never could.

Dubby finally received a call from a serious buyer, after ignoring four hagglers. He rushed to the door, promising he would come back before *the end*. Gwen knew he wouldn't be back, so she rushed to the door and shouted after him before he turned into the lobby and out the front door. She shuffled toward him and he waited impatiently, staring at his smart watch and beginning to perspire.

"What did he do to you?" she asked.

Dubby dropped his fat hands near his sides and sighed. "Look, it's not what Dad did to us, but what he didn't do."

"What does that mean?" Gwen asked with growing frustration, as if the prospect of Donald being negligent would be worse than any accusation of abuse.

"I don't know. We didn't play catch. He wasn't there for advice and when we wound up in trouble he acted as if we hadn't heeded some sort of instruction that he had never offered to us. He just . . . I don't know how to fully explain it. You'll have to ask Aaron when he gets in. He sent me an email that he'd be here soon. I've got to run." He shrugged and answered the call before the caller hung up. Gwen was amazed how easily Dubby could go from dumbfounded by repressed emotions and memories to competent salesmen in only a moment.

ℱↄ

Gwen hummed and whistled away two more afternoons without a visit from Dubby or any sign that Aaron would finally show. Aaron—a mystery to Gwen in many respects, most of all in Donald's refusal to speak of his eldest son—had replied to the email she had sent to both boys with, "Coming. -A." He gave no hints as to when he would arrive or that he even knew where to go, but before sunset of Donald's third day off of his feeding tube, two young boys appeared at the threshold of their small room. They stared wide-eyed, through curly blond bangs, at the many western-themed photos and paintings around the room. Once they noticed Gwen, they sheepishly stepped back into the hallway with their gaze directed at the floor. Their father approached and passed them in the doorway, thanking a nurse for directing them to the correct room.

Aaron entered the room with warmth and cordiality, reminding Gwen of her early years with Donald. He acknowledged the contrast of Gwen's liveliness before his father's decay, but it was clear which had the deepest effect. His boys prepared to follow him in, but he held up a hand, cautioning them. The eldest stopped the younger from moving forward, but he himself peeked around the doorframe at his grandfather. Aaron blew a hot and despairing sigh through his nose. "Dubby, you liar," he whispered to himself. He turned to the boys and gestured them to come in.

The eldest ridded himself of shyness and stepped through the door with his shoulders straight, a confident stride, and clear and attentive eyes. Gwen knew the entrance was well-practiced and passed down faithfully. The younger followed behind, using his older brother as a shield to anything new and different.

"I'm Malachi," the eldest said with the strongest and deepest tone he could muster, offering his hand to Gwen.

Gwen shook Malachi's wiry, strong grip and smiled. "Delighted, young man," she said, giving him a title that he was sure to enjoy. The younger boy rooted his nose into his brother's back and shrank his figure so as not to be seen.

"Be your own man, Uriah," Aaron commanded his son.

The younger boy obediently stepped out from behind his brother and said, "I'm Uriah Yeats Wister. Nice to meet you, ma'am."

Gwen noticed their introductions were positively southern, but their accents were tinted Yankee. Uriah offered his hand and Gwen shook his as well. It was limp and ready to flee her wrinkly grip. "Likewise, Uriah. I'm Gwen."

The boys said in unison, "Nice to meet you, Mrs. Gwen."

She giggled. "It's been a while since I've been a Missus, but I'll take it!"

"We're indebted," Aaron said without taking his eyes away from his father.

Gwen had avoided looking at Donald as much today. His rigidity and lifeless form hardened further and she thought his time drew near, but the vitals monitor chirped away. Aaron picked up the chair Dubby had sat in, placed it lightly before Donald and Gwen, sat down, and lifted his sons to his thighs. The chair never whined nor popped. The boys poked and prodded each other. Aaron spoke past their play to Gwen. "When did he quit speaking?" he asked.

Gwen stared up at the popcorn ceiling, searching for the answer. "Probably close to two years now. I don't know if that's because he really couldn't speak, or he grew tired of talking to me." She chuckled nervously. "They've told me these situations don't normally carry on so long."

"You're talking about the man who told his sons that building fence was 'a lot of fun.' He was tough before our momma died, but afterward, you could have tipped a bit with him and drilled for oil," Aaron said, looking admiringly toward his father. "You've been with him eight years now?"

"Ten."

"Yes, truly indebted." He lifted his heels rhythmically, bouncing the boys during their war of poking.

"I know I am not family, so forgive me if this is intruding, but when was the last time you spoke to Don—I mean, your father?" Gwen asked and immediately regretted asking.

Aaron's heels stopped and he stared at her as she had stared at Dubby for his many stupid comments. "Do you think he can hear us?" Aaron asked, nodding toward his father.

Gwen sighed from her lower lip, blowing wispy bangs away from her eyes. "I like to think he can hear me. I also like to think he can see all the paintings I've made him."

Aaron tussled each of his sons' hair and squeezed them close to his chest. "Malachi just turned seven, so I'd say it has been close to eleven years now."

A year before me, Gwen thought, *no wonder he was in such a state when we met.*

Aaron continued, "It wasn't our best conversation. It ended with me leaving less gracefully than I had wished. He thought he had thrown me off, but I was leaving anyway."

"Why?" Gwen asked.

"We prefer Atlantic cod to Black Angus, don't we, boys?" Aaron bounced both boys.

"Donald wanted you to stay?"

Aaron nodded. "He expected us to own, operate, and enjoy *his* life, but he couldn't foresee Dubby only being useful when he put the ranch up for sale, or that I would want to leave it and a half-finished degree."

"Where is it you live now?"

"Maine. I own a small fleet of commercial fishing boats. I was attracted to the water at a young age. You can imagine how I felt that the nearest shorelines were two farm ponds and a flood control." Aaron chuckled and then immediately appeared dejected. "I never despised my home or where I came from, but I didn't want to stay. Dad never believed that both could be true."

Though Gwen was fascinated by Aaron's warmth and forthrightness, her old feelings toward him for never returning and mending things while Donald could still communicate were re-kindled. "But, to never return, to never speak to him until . . . until he . . ." She couldn't finish without breaking. "I saw how it affected him to not hear from you or see you. I figured out your birthday by the way he would retreat to harder and harder work for a few days. He yearned for *you*."

The boys' poking eased. Malachi began to listen more intent-ly, but Uriah continued his pestering. Aaron smiled and shook his head. "You misunderstand, Gwen. He yearned for what he *wanted* me to be. 'If you come home a fisherman, you should never come home.' That's what he told me before I left with Cheyenne. He wouldn't even come to the wedding that we had here in town."

"You couldn't have stayed? You couldn't have run the place at least until Dubby was fit enough to take over?" Gwen felt as if she pleaded and begged with a young Aaron that had been molded and set long ago.

"There's always room for 'I could have done this' or 'I could have done that'. I went to Maine to provide for my wife's education. By the time she graduated, I had two boats to run, Malachi here, and her parents were living with us."

"I see," Gwen muttered. It was plain to her that both Donald and Aaron carried a weight of responsibility in what had been broken, but it was unclear to her which of them actually deserved that weight. Neither ever gave her an idea who had broken the relationship with such permanence and irreconcilability. She knew Donald's stubbornness firsthand and began to grow in the knowl-edge of Aaron's desire to go his own way. Maybe they had both sinned against each other. The more she thought of it the more she admired both of them for covering the other's sin in silence.

Aaron laughed a loud and spontaneous laugh, startling his sons and Gwen. He saw their confused expressions and explained through deep chuckles, "There was this one time, about five months after I left, I tried to write to him and come back. Cheyenne and I had been fighting over one of my boneheaded money blunders and I asked Dad for his blessing to come home without mention-ing anything about the fight. He wrote back a few weeks later with this one line. He said . . ." Aaron burst into uncontrollable laughter and gradually composed himself. "He said, 'You married her. So learn to be a husband to her, dumbass.'"

Gwen giggled and blushed. She heard Donald's baritone and brash voice speak the curse as Aaron said it.

"Don't repeat that," Aaron said to his sons. The boys giggled and resumed their poking war.

"They're handsome," Gwen said of the boys without their notice.

"Thank you," Aaron said. "I'm just thankful they're fed and washed. I can always credit Cheyenne for that and so much more."

They both sat silent for a time and watched as the boys developed a counting system for their game, which Malachi inevitably won. Uriah became more and more curious about the shriveled figure in the wheelchair and Malachi refused to look upon what he knew was there.

Uriah couldn't bottle his curiosity any longer. "What's his name?" he asked.

Aaron smiled and looked knowingly at Gwen. "He's Grandpa Wister. He's my daddy that I've told you about."

"Why's he always smiling?" Uriah asked.

Malachi glared at his little brother, still refusing to look upon his grandfather. "He's sick, dumba—"

Aaron smacked Malachi's thigh before he could finish the curse. Malachi squealed and moaned over the reddening fingerprints on his thigh. "What do you tell your brother?"

Tears trickled down Malachi's pallid cheeks. "I—I'm s—sorry, Uriah."

Uriah, saddened by his brother's glare and tone more than his curse, recuperated. "It's okay, Malachi."

"Now to Mrs. Gwen," Aaron said sternly.

"I'm sorry, Mrs. Gwen."

"It's forgiven, Malachi. Boys that seek forgiveness quickly become men." Gwen smirked at Malachi. Malachi turned his eyes toward his lap and sulked.

"I asked at the desk and they said he'd been without the tube for three days. When is it . . . can he . . . have you heard how long?" Aaron asked tenderly.

"It was only supposed to be two days or so, but now I'm thinking it could be weeks."

"And he's basically . . ."

"Starving." The strength and curtness with which Gwen spoke surprised her. "Sorry, sometimes I think of these things so much they just become easy to say and hear."

This was no consolation to Aaron, who's eyes bleared and lips quivered under his bite. "Boys," Aaron said and pointed at Donald's wasting figure, "that is the man who taught me what honor is. He taught me about virtue and work. He taught me many of the things I teach you now. He taught me to love my neighbor."

"Like Mrs. Quimby?" Malachi interrupted.

"Yes, like Mrs. Quimby. He taught me to love your mommy."

Uriah squirmed under his father's arm. "Where is Mommy?" he whined.

"She's taking care of Phil. We'll see Mommy soon. Your Grandpa taught me to respect creatures."

"I miss Solo," Malachi groaned.

Aaron smiled through tears at Gwen. "Solo is our German Shepherd." He looked back at his father, forcing his eyes to focus on the man as he had been and reminding himself of these words as he spoke them to his sons. "He taught me a few of the things that will continue without him. I pray I can use and teach you the whole counsel of those things that will continue on without me."

Aaron wept over his alarmed boys. Gwen, knowing this grief should remain foreign to them for some time, took the boys into the hallway and left Aaron alone with Donald. She led the boys outside on the scant lawn and warned Uriah to avoid the Virginia creeper vines as Donald departed.

৽৯

July's baked clay must be watered in the early hours before dawn or late evening after dusk, if digging a deep grave is required. The Lopez family, the Mexican family that bought Wister Ranch, employed their youngest son as gravedigger. He wore the weariness of his early rising and stood by while the pallbearers, which consisted of Aaron, Dubby, and the Lopez men, lowered Donald's casket next to his late wife's white marble headstone. Her epitaph was stained pink with dust. The Presbyterian minister, who had to travel from a county over, finished his gospel-riddled eulogy and narrowly escaped Dubby's sales pitch on "why ministers should drive SUVs." Gwen stood close to the boys, who were somber but grew less and less somber the deeper the casket was lowered. Gwen did not cry this afternoon. She had cried many times over the years that she had devoted to Donald as he withered, but never in front of him and she wasn't going to begin the practice today.

The grave was filled in what felt like a few moments. The Lopez's and Aaron's clothes were soaked through, but Dubby leaned against a nearby pin oak with only a damp collar, having never grabbed his shovel.

The Lopez patriarch said, "We thank God for this man," and walked away. His sons followed him to his Ford. They all piled in and barreled through the pasture toward the dirt road that led back to the ranch house. The youngest clung to the squeaking tailgate with a white-knuckled grip that was visible across the pasture.

"Hold on, little buddy!" Cheyenne strained her whisper. She looked worryingly at the boy and his bouncing shovel. Her bleached blond curls were packed tightly in a bun, opposite her pointed chin. Her youngest son, Philemon, cooed in her arms. "I know it's hot, Phil. I know. I know."

Gwen had only been around the little family for three short days, but she loved them. She even wondered if she should give Donald a post-mortem chiding for sending his son away like he had. She knew Donald's stubbornness would have easily shrugged off her objections.

Aaron approached them, his chest heaving and brow pointed down, away from the sun's glare. He kissed Cheyenne's lips lightly. He bore the entire weight of burying a father that had turned him away and was careful to let no one but himself carry it. He squatted and met the eyes of Malachi and Uriah. He gave them a smile he had practiced, believing it was part of their inheritance and wishing it had been part of his own. He gripped and hugged them as an extra measure of love in his legacy. He stood and moved toward Gwen. He took her hand between his palms and tremored gently, much like Donald's first tremors. She panicked for a moment, but remembered the work he had just done, the heat, and his lack of sleep.

"Cheyenne and I were talking last night about you. We know you don't have any plans after this," he said.

Gwen smiled. "That's a nice way of putting it."

"We want you to come home with us," Aaron said.

"Oh, stop that! You don't owe me anything. I loved Donald and I never expected a dime from him or you."

Aaron shook his head slowly. "That's not what we were thinking. It would help us just as much as it would help you." He started to cry, though his voice was thick and steady like pouring cream. "The boys don't have any grandparents left. We have neighbors, but it's not the same. You know. It's just not the same."

"How do you know I'm not some sort of crazy old woman?" she said, trying to play away from his sincerity.

But his sincerity intensified. "I know you are. If you lived with that man," he pointed to the fresh soil and smiled, "for five of his speaking years, then you're definitely crazy. It's going to take all the crazy you have to live with these boys."

Gwen looked down on the blond sprites. She had resolved not to cry over Donald anymore, but his grandchildren were another matter entirely. Her eyes dried somewhere over Ohio.

§